Zara needed no man in her life. Unless it was Garrick. He needed no woman. Unless it was *her*. Both of them were in the fierce grip of an obsession that had at its core a fatal flaw.

There could be no real love, no real future, without *trust*.

She could never hope to make him trust her again. He had never read a single *one* of her letters. The pain of it seared her so badly she doubted she would ever mention those letters again. Her father was dead. She couldn't confront him, make him confess to Garrick what he had said and done to drive them apart.

THE RYLANCE DYNASTY

The lives & loves of Australia's most powerful family

Growing up in the spotlight hasn't been easy, but the two Rylance heirs, Corin and his sister Zara, have come of age and are ready to claim their inheritance.

Though they are privileged, proud and powerful, they are about to discover that there are some things money can't buy…

In July you met Corin Rylance in:

AUSTRALIA'S MOST ELIGIBLE BACHELOR

This month it's Corin's sister Zara Rylance's story!

CATTLE BARON NEEDS A BRIDE

BY
MARGARET WAY

Margaret Way, a definite Leo, was born and raised in the subtropical River City of Brisbane, capital of the Sunshine State of Queensland. A Conservatorium-trained pianist, teacher, accompanist and vocal coach, she found her musical career came to an unexpected end when she took up writing—initially as a fun thing to do. She currently lives in a harbourside apartment at beautiful Raby Bay, a thirty-minute drive from the state capital, where she loves dining *al fresco* on her plant-filled balcony, overlooking a translucent green marina filled with all manner of pleasure craft: from motor cruisers costing millions of dollars, and big, graceful yachts with carved masts standing tall against the cloudless blue sky, to little bay runabouts. No one and nothing is in a mad rush, and she finds the laid-back village atmosphere very conducive to her writing. With well over one hundred books to her credit, she still believes her best is yet to come.

CHAPTER ONE

THIRTY minutes out of Brisbane, dark silver-shafted clouds, billowing like an atomic mushroom, began to roll in from the east. A veteran of countless flying hours, he watched in familiar fascination as the pluvial masses began to bank up in spectacular thunder heads that spiralled into the stratosphere. Nature at its awesome best, he thought; unimaginable power that could pick up a light plane, roll it, drop it, strike it with lightning, or miraculously allow it to pass through.

This afternoon's pyrotechnic show was one he knew he could handle. But spectacular or not, a line of raging thunderstorms wasn't what he needed right now. He felt a knot of frustration tighten in his chest. Abominable weather inspired trepidation in any pilot but he hadn't got the luxury of giving into it. The Baron nosed into the dense grey fog. It closed in on all sides like a wet, heavy blanket, swallowing the aircraft up. Streams of tarnished silver shot through with silent lightning like tracer bullets flew past the wings.

He couldn't accept another disruption to his long journey in stoic silence. He let out a few hearty curses that steadied head and hand, effectively reducing the build-up of tension. As the man behind the controls, he had to remain passive. It was the only way to stay in command.

He was an experienced pilot. It was a long time since he had gained his licence—as it happened, immediately he was eligible. His father, Daniel, had been so proud of him, clapping a congratulatory hand on his shoulder.

"You're a natural, Garrick. You do everything with such ease. I couldn't be more proud of you, son!"

Surely the answer lay in inherited skills? His father had been his role model for everything. He had taken to flying the same way his father had. Naturally. But he was no fly-by-the-seat-of-your-pants pilot. He was meticulous. Flying was the stuff of life for him. It was also the stuff of death. He could never forget that. Not for a moment. There had been far too many light aircraft crashes in the Outback. Yet he loved flying with a passion! The roar down the runway, then lifting up like an eagle into the wild blue yonder with only the clouds for company. The incredible *freedom* of it! It was marvellously exhilarating and marvellously peaceful at one and the same time. Yet over the years he had flown through countless bad and often frightening situations. One need only consider the perilous weather—far worse than what he was encountering now—over the stifling hot and humid immensity of the Top End savannahs in the middle of the wet season!

His brief moment of frustration over, he found fresh energy, bringing his concentration to bear on winding the plane in and out of a series of down draughts, the sort that always left passengers seriously sick and shaking; there was comfortable seating for four passengers aft. But, for him, there was a weird kind of rush negotiating the thermal traffic. The Beech Baron was a beautiful machine—a symbol of what his pioneering family had attained—from the twin Continental engines to the state-of-the-art avionics. The Baron was religiously maintained to keep it as safe and airworthy as humanly possible. Even so, at one point severe turbulence began to toss the 2500 kilogram aircraft around like a kid's toy. Mercifully, it cut out before it became a real nuisance.

All in all it had been one hell of a trip. First up, he had agreed to take on a medical emergency flight for a neighbouring station owner who had been without wings for some time. Big financial setbacks were the cause he knew. It was his grandfather, Barton, who had made Rylance Enterprises one of the first pastoral companies to diversify to the extent that Coorango was only one of a number of major income earners. The dicey situation that had faced Garrick on this flight was to land on a sealed Outback road. A road that cut through the middle of the uninhabitable wilds: risky at the best of times, given the width of the road and the danger the kangaroos in the area posed. Kangaroos were easily spooked by noises, never mind the hellish din made by the descending Beech Baron's engines. Generally they went into a blind panic, hopping all over the road and near vicinity, presenting a range of hazards. Some would plonk down on an airstrip as if overtaken by acute arthritis, turning soft dark glossy eyes that said, *don't hurt me*. Kangaroos didn't do common sense well.

At least there had been no danger of the makeshift airstrip being too short. The bush highway went on into infinity, cutting a straight path through a fiery rust-red landscape densely sown with billowing clumps of spinifex bleached a burnt gold, stunted shrubs with branches like carvings, innumerable dry watercourses that the nomadic Aborigines used as camps and here and there life saving waterholes that gleamed a molten gold in the sunlight.

Sand. Spinifex. Claypans. Such was the Interior.

The station hand, poor guy, had been grey-faced, sweating, in all sorts of agony. Not that to his everlasting credit, he uttered a single word of complaint. At best guess, a gall or kidney stone. The station owner and two of his men had brought the patient by ute to the highway, where they'd loaded him aboard the Beech Baron on a stretcher. It was his self-imposed task to fly the man to the nearest RFD Base. The Royal Flying Doctor Service at that particular point in time was pushed to the limit with an unusually high number of young mothers going into labour and all kinds of serious station injuries, like having a shoulder run through by a bull's horn for one. Apparently the poor beggar had been pinned to the rail for a good twenty minutes.

His Good Samaritan act had set back his time log. He didn't think he deserved the barrage of thanks he had received from the grateful group.

"You're a marvel, you are, Rick, old son!" Scobie, the station owner, a giant of a man with the girth of a beer barrel, had slapped his back in admiration. A lesser man would have lost his balance and toppled to the ground. *"Takes one hell of a pilot to land a Beech Baron worth well over a million dollars, dead square at 180ks on a bush highway. Can't thank you enough, mate. Whitey here had his eyes covered the whole time you were landing!"* Scobie looked across at the whipcord-lean stockman, who grinned sheepishly.

"Never seen nuthin' like it, Mr Rylance!" volunteered Whitey. *"Word is, you're an ace!"*

"An ace with a lot of luck, Whitey!"

By the time he reached Brisbane, the storm was over as if it had never been. A brazen brassy sun slanted through the massed cloud display, swiftly dispersing it. The sky was washed a vigorous opal-blue. It was coming on to sunset, the usual tropical glory, but soon after the indigo dusk of the tropics would fall like a curtain. He landed the aircraft as smoothly as any blue crane landing on water, parking it behind a Gulfstream jet. Time would come when he'd get around to buying one outright himself. After flight checks were done, he disembarked from the plane, making his way across the concrete apron to the chauffeur driven limousine waiting to take him to the Rylance riverside mansion.

"Good flight, Mr Rylance?" the chauffeur asked, tipping two fingers to the smart grey cap of his uniform.

"I've had better." He smiled, keeping his hand on his one piece of luggage, a large suitcase which he swung into the boot. He didn't need the chauffeur to do it for him, for goodness' sake.

A moment more and they were underway, keeping to pleasant small talk. The purpose of his long journey was to act as best man for his kinsman, Corin, at his wedding in two days' time. This was to be a great occasion after the extremely traumatic months following the deaths of Dalton Rylance, Corin and Zara's father, and his glamorous second wife, Leila in a plane crash in China. It was an event that had shocked the nation. Dalton Rylance had been an industrial giant. But life went on and one had no recourse but to go with it. Or go under. Corin was a warrior. He was now to receive his reward, marrying the love of his life, Miranda Thornton.

Garrick had met petite, silver-blonde Miranda at Dalton's funeral and taken to her immediately. Not only was she enchanting to look at, she was highly intelligent— she planned to become a doctor—so that engaging manner might come in handy at some patient's bedside. Corin was lucky. And deserved to be. Life hadn't been easy for him, or Zara either, after the premature death of their mother, the first Mrs Rylance, universally adored by the extended family. Not so the second Mrs Rylance. She certainly hadn't won his mother's heart. Garrick's mother from time to time had a scathing tongue. He had met Leila on isolated family occasions and found her unexpectedly warm and charming. Or at least she had turned on the charm which she had in abundance for him.

"You're a rich, handsome young man, my darling." His mother had offered an astringent explanation. *"Goes a long way with women like Leila."*

Be that as it may, Leila Rylance had been a stunningly glamorous woman and she had made the arrogant and demanding Dalton happy. So, tragedy all round. Even the super-rich couldn't escape it.

Dalton Rylance and *his* father Daniel had been second cousins. His own branch of the family had been sheep and cattle barons since colonial days. His father was a wonderful man, a truly inspirational figure and a hero to his family. Tragically, for the past few years he had lived out his life in a wheelchair after suffering severe spinal injuries in a riding accident, caused when he went to the assistance of a foolhardy jackeroo on the station.

Dalton and Daniel had never been close, though his father held a substantial block of shares in Rylance Metals. Dalton Rylance had not been a man who inspired liking, never mind affection, but he had been a brilliant business-man, a larger than life character and a major pioneer of the State's mining industry.

As happened far more often than he cared to dwell on, Garrick's thoughts turned to Zara. She who had abandoned him to an emotional hell. Once upon a time, he and Zara had been passionately in love. Correction. *He* had been passionately in love. Zara had been spreading her wings. Trying out her prolifically blossoming womanly powers in sexual exploration. Their lovemaking had lifted his heart clear of his body. He had been *wild* for her. He would have done *anything* for her. Made any sacrifice, short of abdicating his inheritance. He had always known, as his father's only son and heir he had huge responsibilities waiting for him—just as did Corin, Dalton's heir.

Zara was the Rylance heiress. Dalton, the quintessential chauvinist, had expected little else of her than to look beautiful and in time marry the scion of another enormously rich family and produce heirs. Dalton Rylance had carried the banner loudly proclaiming that women had no head for business.

"Big business can only be run by men."

Predictably, Rylance Metals was male orientated. So, for that matter, was Rylance Enterprises, though that was fast changing. His mother, Helen, sat on the board of all of their companies, taking an *active* not passive role. It was she who had recommended, then had brought in another two key businesswomen who had proved their worth. His mother was quite a woman. And a great judge of character, which had often made him often wonder how she had slipped so badly with Zara.

His beautiful, beautiful Zara. His dark angel. The stuff of dreams.

At twenty-eight, two years younger than he, she was still unattached when everyone had thought she would marry early and brilliantly. Any young woman as beautiful and radiant as Zara, let alone an heiress, would attract a great deal of male attention. She had never been without her long line of admirers. Only, to her credit, Zara was no spoilt little rich girl. She had turned herself into a high-flyer in the business world. Dalton hadn't reckoned on his only daughter's cleverness. But Zara had inherited the Rylance business brain. Even so, Dalton had never offered her a job within Rylance Metals.

One of his few *big* mistakes. But then Dalton Rylance had been a man of his time. For some years now Zara, armed with a Masters Degree in Business—Dalton had allowed that to protect the inheritance that was to come to her—had called London her home. That was where she lived and worked. And formed dangerous relationships. Some time back, she had been embroiled in a huge scandal over there. A cause célèbre involving a notorious and extremely rich European businessman, Konrad Hartmann, a man with vast multinational interests, who, after a lengthy undercover operation, had been found guilty of fraud on a massive scale. Hartmann was currently awaiting trial—these things took time—but no doubt he would enjoy the good life in jail, where he could buy plenty of protection. When the story first broke, the less respected section of the British press had dubbed Zara *Hartmann's beautiful young Australian mistress*. The seed, not so subtly planted, was that she could have been privy to Hartmann's dubious and convoluted business dealings, or must have had her suspicions. She was, by all accounts, something of a financial whiz-kid herself as well as the daughter of Australian mining magnate, Dalton Rylance. All grist for the mill! The media had a field day, skating as close to libel as they could.

The threat of legal action had called off the hawks. Zara's distinguished and enormously influential boss at the time, Sir Marcus Boyle, had gone in to bat for her. Corin hadn't wasted any time, flying to London to arrange top legal representation. Later, when things settled, he had brought Zara home. Apparently, she had been all too willing to come.

He found no pleasure in the knowledge that Zara had had her fingers badly burned. An ill-advised love affair with a billionaire white-collar criminal, no less, though she had denied any serious ongoing relationship right from the start. But was that strictly true? Only Zara and Hartmann would know. What *he* knew for a fact was that he would never forgive Zara for how she had treated him. His heart might leap at the sight of her. His eyes might forever be dazzled. But a broken heart didn't easily mend. Heartache more often than not hatched *hatred*. Obsessive relationships were inherently of extremes. Only he didn't have it in him to hate Zara. All he could do was prevent her from ever again finding a chink in his armour.

Part of him had wanted to refuse Corin's invitation to be his best man. As Zara was to be chief bridesmaid, he knew he was taking an almighty risk. Even the sound of her name had the power to hurt him. Not that anyone would ever know. He had become expert at hiding his feelings. In the end, he'd decided he couldn't possibly let Corin down. It was, after all, an honour. Corin didn't know the full story of his betrayal at Zara's hands. Nor would he ever. He and Zara had that secret in common. He and Zara would sit together at the bridal table. Pass for kin on the friendliest of terms.

He had done a lot of living since Zara had fled him. One unsuccessful attempt at putting the past behind him. He and Sally Forbes had become engaged at a big party her parents had thrown for them. The Forbes were a long established pastoral family and close friends. He had known Sally since forever. She was everything a young man in his position should choose. Outback born. A fine equestrienne. Phenomenal energy. Very attractive—lustrous nut-brown hair, dancing hazel eyes, well educated, confident and outgoing. Trained from girlhood to take her place as mistress of some large pastoral establishment. Like Coorango. It might have worked if the thought of Zara and what he had felt for her—what he had felt for a *woman*—hadn't dogged his every step. In the end he and Sally had broken up. She had since married a mutual friend, Nick Draper, some said on the rebound. He hoped not. Sally and Nick remained his friends. Better yet, they looked happy with each other.

"Too much of you goes on inside your head, Rick. I never really know what you're thinking."

He felt bad about that. He couldn't get past Zara. Or the ache in him.

Sometimes he couldn't believe the passage of years. Could it possibly be five? Zara had made an attempt at bridging the deep gulf between them, writing many letters. The latest had been sent from London. That was shortly before she'd started to appear on the front page of the London newspapers. The temptation to read her letters had been powerful. He'd had to wrestle long and hard with the urge to slit the envelopes and devour the contents but he had come to think of it as a betrayal of himself. Of his self-esteem. Accordingly, the letters, tied in a thick bundle and shoved away in the back of a bureau drawer, had finally been consigned, not to the shredder, but *fire*. Fire seemed appropriate.

The past was off-limits.

Such a pity he couldn't erase memory.

CHAPTER TWO

THE Rylance Mediterranean-style mansion was some house. Dauntingly vast, it was set in five acres of landscaped gardens that at the rear led past a turquoise swimming pool and a pool house big enough to hold a family, down to the river, deep, broad and thrillingly dangerous in flood. In spring and summer the banks were overhung by prolifically blossoming trees. The front of the house sat at the centre of a sweeping cul-de-sac with only two very expensive estates to either side.

He had been a boy when he first visited the house. At ten, Outback children—at least those whose parents could afford it—were sent to boarding school to receive the best possible education. It was a tradition. He and Corin had been enrolled at birth in the same prestigious boys' college their fathers and their grandfathers before them had attended. They were to start Grade Five together in the coming year.

His bonding with Corin had been one of those instant things. Friends and kinsmen right from the start. Corin's beautiful little sister, Zara, had appeared to him like the princess in his own little sister Julianne's fairy stories. For one thing, she wore a white dress with embroidery all over it, the like of which he had never seen. Her long gleaming dark hair had been pulled back from her face, held with a wide blue satin ribbon but left to slide like a waterfall over her shoulders and down her back. For Jules, who was six at that time everyday gear was asexual—T-shirts, shorts or jeans, boyish cap of dark curls. That was the norm on the station for all the kids.

He had been irresistibly and utterly captivated by Corin's sister, who even then had dizzying power over him. He had a theory that she had established herself so early and so vividly that it had been impossible for him to see her as she really was. But, for all the excitement and attendant dangers of living on a vast Outback station, meeting little Zara Rylance, a cousin of sorts, had been one of the big moments of his childhood.

"This is Zara, Garrick. My jewel of a daughter!"

Corin and Zara's beautiful mother Kathryn had smilingly introduced them, perhaps amused by his open-mouthed reaction. The little girl, to his astonishment, had sweetly and composedly given him her hand. How graceful was that? How adult!

Of course her mother had taught Zara her polished manners. Kathryn Rylance had been such a gracious woman of luminous poise. Who could possibly have imagined that not all that many years later she would be dead, killed in a spectacular crash when her powerful sports car became airborne and went over a bridge? The entire extended family had been stunned and saddened. He remembered his own strong-minded, highly articulate mother loudly deploring the fact that Dalton Rylance had remarried a relatively short time later.

"Young enough to be his daughter, Daniel, would you believe?" she'd addressed his father, her eyes the deep and brilliant blue she had passed on to her son sparkling in condemnation. *"What is to happen to those children, so deprived of their loving mother? That callous monster*

Dalton will be no comfort at all. Little Zara will be the one to suffer the most. Mark my words. Are you listening to me, Daniel? With Zara around, Dalton and this new Mrs Rylance will never be able to forget Kathryn. I know you don't like my saying it, but I've always believed our dearest Kathy was in such distress—"

At that point his mother, who had gained a reputation for looking ageless, had broken off, quickly swivelling her burnished head.

His father had caught sight of him, hovering at the door, and called out his name. *"It's all right, Garrick. Come in."*

Just as he was hanging on what his mother was about to say! Everyone knew his mother had not been impressed by Leila Rylance. She made no secret of it. In fact she was very outspoken. Not surprising perhaps when she'd had considerable affection for the tragic Kathryn who Zara so closely resembled.

The spectacular hand-forged iron gates, ebony offset with gleaming brass scrolls, parted on command. Then slowly closed behind them. They were cruising up the broad driveway lined by towering Cuban palms. An extraordinarily dramatic display of bromeliads flowered at their feet in long narrow beds that formed an *allee* that reached to the circular drive. Manicured lawns spread away to either side, a lush green never seen in the Outback.

Nearer the mansion, his eyes were enchanted by the sight of the box-edged rose gardens he remembered. The roses, his mother's favourite plant, reigned without attendants. No other plants or under-plantings shared the beds. He approved of that. The rose, after all, was the Queen of Flowers. Now, in early summer, they were in exquisite bloom, each bed devoted to a particular colour—all the pinks from pale to deep, the whites, the yellows and oranges, a hundred iridescent shades of red, crimson, scarlet, ruby, carmine furthest away. The whole aura was one of peace and tranquillity.

He knew Kathryn Rylance had taken great personal interest in the garden. It was she who had worked closely with the head gardener at that time, a transplanted Englishman by the name of Joshua Morris. Josh was a man with a great love and knowledge of roses. It had been his job to enlarge the rose gardens. To no one's surprise, Josh had resigned almost immediately after the news of Kathryn Rylance's death had broken. He was said to have been devastated.

The gardens remained as Kathryn's memorial.

Garrick's fatigue had vanished. Nevertheless, he was acutely aware he was on edge. He wasn't sure whether Zara was staying at the house or not. He knew she had a city apartment. But, with the wedding so close, it was possible she would be staying at the mansion. God knew it could accommodate an army. He understood Zara and Miranda had grown close. But then Zara had enormous charm at her disposal.

Corin had confided he was in two minds about keeping the property. Memories, of course. But, even with any amount of money at his disposal, he would be hard pressed to find a more valuable or better sited property with a superb view of the river to the rear. The estate was a major asset. It had to be worth many millions and state-of-the-art security would already have been put in place by Dalton. It was all up to Corin. Quite possibly, Miranda wouldn't care to live in the house, although she had only met Leila Rylance, the last chatelaine, briefly. Miranda would be in for a lot of exposure as Corin's wife. In the ordinary course of events, medical students didn't get to marry billionaires. From what he had seen of Miranda, he was sure she could hold her own.

He knew, even before the door opened, it would be Zara. That warning tightness in his chest. The first of the shock waves?

Kathryn Rylance had passed on her exquisite features to her daughter. Zara looked up at him with a tremulous smile—no doubt uncertain of his reaction—but her wonderful eyes were already working their spell like some medieval witch. "Hello, Garrick."

Just the sight of her! Did she know how it *hurt*? A thousand electrifying volts of recognition. The accompanying sense of futility for ever having loved someone beyond reach. Would he never get over the tortured angst he had carried around as a young man?

You're carrying a torch you can't put down, let alone put out, you fool.

He was older, wiser. His heartache had morphed into steely resolve. He didn't fully realise it but he was radiating sexual antagonism. "Zara, I wondered if you'd be here."

She flushed at his cutting tone. "I don't expect a hug."

"I'm not a big hugger any more, Zara," he offered very dryly, when his heart was beating like a bass drum. "You cured me of that. Am I allowed to come in?'

"Of course." Her flush deepened, like the pink bloom on a rose. She stood back, a willowy young woman with an entrancingly slender silhouette. Her gleaming dark hair was caught back in some elaborate knot, emphasizing her swan's neck and the set of her pretty ears. She was dressed in a white sleeveless blouse with gauzy ruffles down the front and narrow-legged black pants. Tall as she was, above average in height, she still wore high heeled slingbacks on her feet. A simple enough outfit albeit of the finest quality. Zara enhanced everything she wore.

"Corin's been delayed," she told him, clearly showing her nerves. She had to look up at him. He, like Corin, was inches over six feet. "Miri is with him. Just a quick drink with friends. They'll be home for dinner, which is at seven."

"I remember," he said, slightly relaxing the tension in his voice.

"Shall I show you to your room?"

She gave him another shaky smile. She sounded very gentle, very anxious to please. "Where are the staff?" he asked briskly, as if he would much prefer one of them to do the job.

"They're about. I wanted to greet you myself."

"Really?" He raised a black brow. "I suppose we *do* have to sort out how best to handle the next couple of days.'

His expression must have been harsh because she said, "You still hate me?" Her own expression was one of deep regret.

He didn't have to consider his response. It was automatic. "Don't kid yourself, Zara."

Don't let those big dark eyes drag you in.

"If you ever haunted my dreams, those days are long past."

"You still haunt mine," she said very simply.

Great God! The cheek of her! His answer was so stinging it made her flinch. "You always were good at putting on a show. But surely you're not over Hartmann already?"

She visibly recovered her poise, her tone unwavering. "You're talking utter nonsense, Garrick. I was never

involved with Konrad Hartmann. There was no relationship as such. A few dinner dates. A couple of concerts."

"I guess I can accept that." He shrugged. "Goddesses
don't fall in love with mere mortals. But you had a sexual
relationship?"

"Hardly any of your business," she said with considerable reserve.

"Of course you did."

He glanced away from her beautiful face into the sumptuous formal living room. It had been redecorated since he
had last seen it. Now its palette was gold, turquoise and
citrine-yellow, with the walls painted a shade of terracotta
impossible for him to describe. This grand room had once
been walled in with a graceful curving arch that matched
the arch on the other side. Now both huge reception rooms
were open to the entrance hall.

It was a real coup! In fact it was stunning. The entrance hall remained floored in traditional black and white
marble tiles but, as he lifted his head, he saw the new white
coffered ceiling. In place of the arches, four Corinthian
columns soared to left and right, acting as a splendid
colonnade.

So who had inspired the magic? Some high-priced designer with impeccable taste? Miranda? Very possibly,
Zara. It looked like her—the refinement—he decided. Zara
always did have tremendous style.

She was standing a short distance away, appearing lost
in her own thoughts. "I can't talk about Konrad Hartmann,"
she was saying. "I was the victim there."

He lowered his coal-black head, his expression highly
sceptical. "His beautiful Australian mistress?"

"Believe that, you'll believe anything!" She spoke
tautly. "I was sorry to hear your engagement to Sally

Forbes broke up. I do remember her. She was a very attractive girl. And very *suitable*."

He shrugged. "Well, she's happily married to Nick Draper now. Remember him?"

"I remember your other friend, Nash, better."

"Why wouldn't you?" He laughed, a dry and bitter sound. "Nash fell in love with you as well. One way or the other, you left lasting impressions. Corin must have spent a fortune redecorating the place."

"You like it?"

"Someone has superb taste," he said, lowering his dazzling blue gaze to hers. "Was it Miranda? I would have thought she was too preoccupied with her studies. I greatly admire her ambition, by the way."

"As do we all." She spoke tenderly, as if Miranda were a much loved sister. "Miri and I decided on things together. Of course we had a very talented professional team in as well. We didn't want any reminders of—" She stopped short, biting her lower lip. It was fuller than the sensitive upper lip. She had a beautiful mouth. Once he could have kissed it all day. All night. Pretty well *did*.

"Go on," he urged in a clipped tone, thinking he might never have any real protection against this woman. "You didn't get on with your stepmother, did you? I suppose it's understandable. You couldn't bear another woman to take over from your mother, let alone steal your father's attention away from you."

She put her hand to her throat as though such a charge caused her great pain. "What would you know about it, Garrick?"

"I don't pretend I know a great deal," he confessed. "After all, we've lived over a thousand miles apart for nearly all of our lives. But I do recall your telling me any number of times how Leila had come between you and your father. Not that we spent much time *talking*, or indeed talking about anyone else but ourselves and our plans for a future together," he tacked on with marked bitterness.

"She did more than that," Zara pointed out, keeping her face as expressionless as she could. "But one isn't supposed to speak ill of the dead. Suffice to say, it was Miranda more than anyone who wanted big changes."

"What? Wasn't what was already in place good enough?" he asked in genuine surprise. "No one could say poor tragic Leila lacked style."

Zara half turned away, showing him her lovely profile. "Let's get off the subject, shall we? It's really not your concern."

"Of course it isn't," he agreed suavely. "But, tell me, what exactly *is* my concern?" He picked up his suitcase. "I'm Corin's best man."

"Corin thinks the world of you." She began to lead the way to the double height divided staircase that swirled upward to left and right at the end of the entrance hall.

"The feeling is mutual," he said. His eyes were on her delicate shoulders and straight back. "It's *you* who seriously messed up. By the way—" he paused, wanting to know the answer "—Corin doesn't know about *us*, does he? Or the dubious *us* we were."

She didn't stop, knowing he was baiting her. "No need to bring your suitcase," she said. "Someone will bring it up."

"Just answer the question," he returned curtly.

Now she turned to face him, feeling racked with emotion. His height and strength, the grace and vibrant life. If only one could wish for one's time over again! Had she known it, her eyes, huge and haunting, dominated a magnolia-pale face.

She was the most desirable woman in the world, despite

the way she had treated him, Garrick thought, struggling against a rush of fever and remembered passion.

She messed you up once. Don't let her do it again.

"You didn't read my letters, did you?" she asked sadly, one slender hand holding on to the gleaming brass handrail, as if for support.

Anger was driving him now. He made a grab for it. Got it under control.

Don't let her see she's getting to you.

"What was the point? You were never coming back to me. You made that abundantly clear. You were just spreading your wings. Taking advantage of all I felt for you."

"I was scared of my father," she said, superb actress that she was, managing to still look upset and frightened. "He called. I jumped."

Garrick fired up, his voice like a whiplash "Oh, rubbish! Your father gave you *everything*! You wanted for nothing." He knew he was betraying far too much emotion.

"Only in some ways," she said. Garrick didn't even know the half of it. "Ever since I was a little girl—even when our mother was alive—my father was such a *controlling* man. He controlled *her*." Tears pooled in her beautiful dark eyes. Resolutely, she blinked them back. "I never had the courage to challenge him. That shames me now. I should have been braver. But my father scared strong men witless. You might consider that. Tough business people, not just servants or the like. Only Corin could stand up to him. I had to pay the price for so closely resembling my mother. Corin was the heir. I was the daughter. A nothing person. Daughters were nothing. But he would never forfeit control. You didn't really know my father, Garrick, any more than you knew Leila. You remember her as a charming, super-glamorous woman, warm and friendly. The reality was very different."

"I thought you weren't going to speak ill of the dead," he reminded her harshly. "And you weren't a handful, I suppose?" he challenged. She was standing on the first step. They were almost eye to eye. He could have reached out and pulled her into his arms. "Your father confided he was greatly disturbed and disappointed in the way you did everything in your power to make life extremely unpleasant for your stepmother. Leila, according to him, *and* her, incidentally—though she said little against you—tried over and over to please you, to establish a connection, but you weren't having any. As I say, it was understandable, but don't lay all the blame on Leila, who isn't here to speak for herself."

"Well, it appears she has *you*," she retorted sharply, visibly stung. "You feel my father and Leila were more trustworthy than me?"

"God, yes!" he freely admitted. "Why would they lie? They appeared most sincere. I know there was a lot of conflict." He frowned. "We *all* more or less knew that. Bringing a beautiful, much younger wife into the family was bound to have repercussions."

"It did that." She turned away, as though realizing it would do no good whatever trying to enlist his sympathy. "I'm sorry, but I don't want to talk about it. You've obviously made up your mind. You don't seem to appreciate that you were blessed, Garrick. Both of us might have been born into wealth and privilege but you grew up with wonderful parents. To most people, being the Rylance heiress meant everything was within my grasp. That wasn't so.

Being wealthy carries its own burdens. You know that. One can buy relationships. People want to know you, be seen with you. But one can never buy love. It's not for sale, when love is *everything* in life."

He gave vent to a theatrical groan. "Oh, *please*! I had love for you, Zara. Do you dimly remember that? You didn't want it. I knew at the time I wanted you more than you wanted me, but that was okay. What you gave me filled my life with radiance. Hope for a glowing future. In reality, there was no hope. What you actually did was expose me to a lot of wasteful unhappiness. You weren't worth it. I detest devious, dishonest behaviour above everything."

Colour swept her face in a rosy tide. "Then your memories are distorted. I wasn't playing any game, Garrick."

He found himself gritting his teeth. "Please do shut up, Zara," he said. "We have a history of heartache, but we can't turn this weekend into a battlefield now, can we? What's past is past."

Her gaze turned inward. "What did the American author, Faulkner say? *The past is never dead; it's not even past.* You and Julianne suffered no family traumas like Corin and I did. You had a wonderful mother and father. *Your* father is the loveliest man—I'm hoping to see him. He invited me to Coorango."

That piece of information came like a king hit *"What?"* He couldn't control the fierceness of his tone. He went after her, taking hold of her arm. And there it was again. The zap of electricity that raised the short hairs on his nape. His eyes blazed, bluer than the finest back-lit sapphires. "Dad *couldn't* have done that without telling me."

"He's still master of Coorango, isn't he?" she challenged, her whole body trembling in his grasp. "Your mother would like to see me too," she swept on. "Helen and I always did get on. She loved my mother. She told me so."

That, at least, was true. For an instant he felt as though his structured life was imploding. "And when is this supposed to be happening?" he rapped, releasing her as though her touch burned him. Which, indeed, it did.

She spread the long pale fingers of her hands. "I think they thought—please be calm, Garrick—"she begged, "—I could fly back with you."

"You can't be serious." He spoke flatly. "Neither of them said a word of this to me." Shock was enveloping him. His parents told him everything. There were no secrets. They had been invited to the wedding as a matter of course. Only his father wasn't anywhere near well enough for the long journey and his mother wouldn't leave her adored husband. Perversely, he now realised some part of him *wanted* Zara to come, amply demonstrating his stupidity where she was concerned.

"So there's a story behind this, is there?" he accused her. "You *asked* could you come. My parents wouldn't refuse you. No doubt Coorango is as far away as you can get. I suppose people are still talking about your involvement with Hartmann."

She moved swiftly away from him to the first landing. A portrait of a very elegant auburn-haired woman in a pink silk gown, late nineteenth century, hung on the wall directly behind her, a stunning backdrop. "A section of the media did their best to destroy me. Mud sticks. I have to live with it. But no one who knows me or loves me doubts my word. Konrad's vast business dealings were under suspicion for a long time. We all knew that. But it took a lengthy, painstaking undercover operation to reveal the truth."

"Look, I don't want to hear about your conman ex-lover. Let's go upstairs," he said dismissively, picking up his suitcase again.

"Of course."

They didn't speak until she stopped outside a bedroom door a distance down the wide corridor, hung with more valuable gilt-framed paintings. Antique chairs and tall Chinese porcelain vases atop carved mahogany stands were set at intervals.

"I hope you'll be comfortable here." She opened the door, gesturing with a graceful movement of her arm that he should go in.

"Nice," he muttered. It was way better than *nice*. The bedroom was large—and he was used to *large*—with a lofty ceiling opening onto the massive plant-filled rear terrace. There was a wrought iron setting where one could get a great view over the rear garden, the swimming pool area and, of course, the deep river. Inside, classic, sophisticated custom furnishings; king-size bed, colour scheme elegantly subdued—cream, bronze, ivory. "The most harmonious bedroom any male guest could ask for," he said without looking at her. He was so close to her his muscles were tensed like steel springs.

"There's an en suite, of course."

"Of course!" he echoed with sarcasm.

She gave him a long searching look. "You've become very hard, haven't you, Garrick?" she said, studying his superbly lean figure. Hardened or not, he was more devastatingly handsome than ever. The heat in his brilliantly blue eyes made her feel consumed. "You've quite lost your smile." He had such a beautiful dazzling smile, like sunshine breaking out.

"Only with *you*, Zara," he shot back with easy mockery.

"Your voice is deeper too," she continued. "You sound

more and more like your father. Once I used to think *Rick will be like that*, with all your father's gravitas and wisdom. His wonderful sense of humour and his under-standing of human nature, our strengths and our weak-nesses. Now, I'm not so sure."

"I'll never be my father," he said. "But I try my best. I never knew *you*, Zara," he countered. "I fell for you when we were kids, outlandish as that may seem. I thought you were as beautiful on the inside as you are on the outside. I was *so* wrong. Anyway, it's all ancient history now. A man can only afford to make a fool of himself once."

"Did you not love Sally at all?" she asked with a serious questioning look.

His blue eyes raked her. "Do you *really* want to know?"

"Very much. I only ever wanted your happiness, Garrick."

He gave her a glower that would have outdone Jane Austen's Mr Darcy. He had developed a real talent for it. Sadly, the glower was intensely sexy.

"Zara, give me a break," he groaned. "You cared *nothing* for me. You were just wallowing in a young man's worship. Sally was a breath of fresh air after you. It was mutual, our breaking up."

Her great eyes flashed prior knowledge. "Not what I heard."

Someone was bound to have told her. "Sally deserved a different kind of partner," he said. "I admit I have grown... harder. Sally needed someone who would suit her better— Nick. So put me in the picture. For a woman who was expected to marry early and brilliantly, you're damned near on the shelf. What happened to all the guys *before* Hartmann?" His expression could have stripped her to the bone.

"No one measured up to you!"

He was so angry he spun about and caught her by the shoulders, shocking himself with the violence of his reaction. He wanted to pick her up bodily. He wanted to… damn…damn…damn…

"Don't *do* this, Zara," he warned. "I'm not sure what lies at the centre of this new campaign—if that's what it is—but, I have to tell you, you disgust me."

She stared back at him with absolute calm. That was a major point in Zara's favour. She could keep her calm. "Feels good, does it, shaking me?"

Instantly he dropped his hands. God, around Zara he needed a keeper. "I'm sorry," he muttered. "You'd do well not to provoke me. Which you're doing deliberately." He could feel the heat running along his arms to his shoulders, down the length of his body. The slightest physical contact and he was on the verge of losing it. He wanted to pull her back into his arms. Kiss her senseless…

For God's sake, remember all you've learned.

Not easy when his emotions were in chaos. Another shock to absorb. For the first time in a long time he had come *alive* in a way he hadn't experienced since she had left him. The powerful sexuality that was in him, so long dormant, was frantic to break free. Now the big question was—just how long was he going to be able to hold out? Weddings were very special occasions. Weddings did things to people. They filled the air with magic. He would have to spend the entire time smothering his instincts to death.

She had slipped one hand to her shoulder, massaging it gently.

Shame overwhelmed him. "I didn't mean to hurt you," he apologised again, not fully aware how daunting his physical presence was—a stunningly fit male, well over six feet, emanating a fierce anger.

"I think you did," she said, but in a low accepting voice. "It's going to be very difficult these next few days if we can't appear to be friends."

He couldn't help it. He threw back his head and hooted, the sound mocking and derisive. *"Friends?"*

"Maybe not—" she wavered in the face of his contempt "—but we're both adults. Surely we can play the part?"

He shrugged a languid shoulder. "I don't see why not. You're a superb actress, and the last thing I want to do is upset Corin and his lovely bride. What I *don't* see is why you want to come back with me to Coorango? I've made it quite clear what I think of you."

Her midnight-dark eyes were pinned to his face. "I haven't seen your parents for some time. *They* like me. They want to see me even if you don't. I admit I'd like to get out of town for a while. Your father and mother understand that. You'll be out and about the station for most of the time. I know how hard you work. I can only say I'll do my best to keep out of your way. I could be a help to your mother, with Jules in Washington, expecting a baby." Julianne Rylance had married a young career diplomat some years back. His current posting, an upgrading, was in Washington.

"I have to think about this," he said. It came from the depths of his being. Take her back to Coorango? Kill or cure? His whole attitude was forced, that was the worst part. A defence mechanism; a way of controlling his emotions. "I like my life the way it is," he told her, not bothering to keep the anger away. "I don't want you back in it. Leave me alone, Zara. Whatever was between us, it's long over."

* * *

The "friendship", curiously enough, lasted right through a delicious dinner and well after. They retired with coffee to the rear terrace, where the river breeze was circulating, shaking out all the myriad scents of the garden. The sky was ablaze with brilliantly blossoming stars. The exterior lights lit the grounds—the huge sapphire pool and the landscaped gardens with their spectacular banks of densely blue hydrangeas, a flower his mother loved but could not grow on Coorango. Even at the rear of the house the air was infused with the fragrance of the roses that mingled with the familiar scent of Zara he was drawing in.

He didn't have to force his smooth easy manner. It came without effort. He was, after all, well schooled and the happiness Corin and Miranda so obviously felt flowed very sweetly and calmingly over him. It lifted his spirits and lowered his entrenched cynicism. Corin adored his Miranda. Miranda adored him. A man should be so lucky!

But then hadn't he once thought the gates of Paradise had been opened to him? Zara had seduced him with all her ravishing little overtures. Or had he seduced her? Who could tell which way it had been? He had made love to her over and over so passionately. She had let him. Or had it been the other way around? Whatever way it had happened, it was as though it was meant to be. Cruel as the outcome had been, he would remember it all his life.

Tonight, both young women were wearing ankle-length summery dresses that fell from shoestring straps. Maxi dresses, Miranda told him when he complimented her on her enchanting appearance. Miranda's dress was in a beautiful stand-out turquoise to match her amazing eyes; Zara's was closely patterned all over with pink and coral flowers outlined in black. Two beautiful young woman, perfect foils for one another. It was clear Zara had worked her charm on her soon-to-be sister-in-law. Miranda's manner with Zara was soft with affection.

Pity she didn't use her winning ways on the tragic Leila.

Zara turned her head. Their eyes met. He took a deep breath that was like a knife thrust. He realised, too late, he had just been sitting there *staring* at her.

A million miserable damns!

He couldn't change how she affected him.

He couldn't unmake the past.

Ecstasy and betrayal often went hand in hand.

Workmen were swarming all over the grounds when he went down to do a few quick laps of the pool. It was a magnificent blue and gold day with the prediction of plenty more perfect days to come. A great omen for the wedding. He woke in the pre-dawn, as was his habit, but for the initial few seconds he couldn't think where he was. His dreams had been anything but restful. Predictably filled with a Zara who kept walking steadily away from him up a rising slope. She was even managing to dominate his unconscious. At one point in the early hours he had woken with one hell of a start, thinking her body was curled around his.

How crazy could a man get?

Getting through the wedding was going to be a lot tougher than he'd thought. The trick was to focus on Corin and his beautiful Miranda and forget his own problems. He wasn't proud of the fact that the woman who had betrayed him still had immense power over him. No wonder men got so angry when they were treated like fools.

By the time he pulled himself out of the pool two splendid white marquees had been erected, with a third underway. Buffet tables were being put swiftly in place with several women waiting to drape them with white damask tablecloths and, he understood, gold moire over-cloths to match the elegant gilt chairs. Excitement was in the air. No doubt about it. He had never seen Corin happier. That counted for a lot.

He was towelling himself off when Zara surprised him by materialising at his shoulder. He hadn't heard her. He'd been too busy watching the proceedings as she had come across the plush emerald grass.

"You were up early," she said, slipping off her flimsy cobalt blue and white cover-up and placing it neatly around the back of a chair.

"Wow!" It came without volition. For a few moments arousal closed his throat.

"Wow?" she questioned, raising her brows.

"Yes, wow, wow, wonderful wow!" he said shortly, angry with himself for making any comment. He felt the predictable blood rush to his loins; more heat from the sight of her than the sun. There was an element of déjà vu in it too. How many times had he and Zara swum together in Coorango's Blue Lady Lagoon? Sometimes with swimsuits, sometimes without. Acting wild. He could still visualise her naked body, her long black hair streaming down her back, creamy skin that never tanned, huge eyes locked on his, each hypnotised by the other.

I love you, Rick. I always will!

And I adore you! We're perfect together.

Every atom of his being—his whole psyche—had told him it was true. Zara was the only girl in the world he wanted to marry.

But that was another time. Another place. Only deep, deep memories would never fade.

"Well, thank you," she said and smiled. "You don't look so bad yourself." A priceless piece of understatement.

"Hard work tends to keep one in shape," he snapped.

"Still tanned all over?"

"That you'll never know."

"Don't make statements that might be used against you," she said softly.

"And don't you try flirting with me," he warned. "You've had your day. Full stop."

"And every day since I've died a little."

He swung on her then, blue eyes blazing.

"Okay, okay!" She held up the palms of her hands in surrender, head held high and proud. "I disgust you. But you haven't found anyone. Neither have I."

"Maybe we damaged one another. Leave it, Zara."

Showing a little agitation she withdrew a long hairpin from her hair; the sun made it gleam, like a thoroughbred's coat polished high for a race. What a glorious thing was a woman's mane, thick and sleek and straight. Her white one-piece swimsuit was cut high at the leg to make the most of her beautiful graceful limbs. The plunging halter neckline revealed a tantalizing glimpse of the sides of her small but perfectly shaped breasts. The top section of the swimsuit was printed with cobalt blue and silver. Plunging neckline or not, she projected her innate refinement and elegance.

He forced himself to look away. He picked up his discarded towel, giving his thick hair a vigorous once over.

"You're not going, are you?" She raised a hand to block the sun from her eyes.

"I've had my swim." He wouldn't look at her.

"Stay, please," she begged. "Miri is coming down. It will make her happy to see us together. You know—*friends*."

His eyes shot over her then, narrowing, intensely blue against his darkly tanned skin. "Ex-lovers. Friends has nothing to do with it. Anyway, I thought I fulfilled my obligations last night."

"We had a lovely time," she said, more a statement than a question.

"And you were so *sweet*," he mocked. "I'm supposed to feel good?"

"Well, at least you *look* good." Her face softened. She gave a little shaky laugh. "Here's Miri now. Please stay on a while, Garrick."

"Okay, I will, for Miranda's sake. Her New Zealand family are arriving before lunch, aren't they?" He ran a hand through his hair, quickly drying in deep crisp waves. A slight frown appeared on his forehead. "I didn't even know until last night that Miranda *had* a family in New Zealand. But then I know very little about her. I even had the notion that side of her family was darn near a closed topic." He gave her a searching look, not all that surprised when she turned her beautiful head away from him. It seemed to him—he could be wrong—there was a story there.

"Well, her distinguished grandfather will be giving her away and her cousin Isabel will be one of the bridesmaids. There *was* a family rift. Sadly, that went on for many years, but all's well now. That's the main thing."

"I guess it is," he agreed, "but there's a lot you're not telling me. Broad outline. Not enough detail."

"Why would you say that?" She spoke too quickly, too intensely. A dead giveaway.

"Zara!" He stopped her with a look. "I can read you like a book. Anyway, leave it for now. I very much like Miranda. Corin is a lucky man."

CHAPTER THREE

EVERYTHING went exactly as planned. The church ceremony was so beautiful, so much a celebration of the
heart, many a married woman abandoned herself to a
gentle nostalgic tear that often escaped onto the cheek,
while the young and the not so young but ever hopeful
vowed to make up for lost time and get working towards
achieving a magical wedding of their own. As an occasion, nothing could beat a wedding. This one was *glorious*,
a real fairy tale affair, the legendary once in a lifetime.
Excitement was running high. Great swirls of genuine
emotion, impossible to describe, but it enveloped them
all. At least for a time.

Miranda was the living fulfilment of the radiant bride.
Her whole countenance, her extraordinary turquoise eyes,
shone with love and joy. Here was a bride her groom could
worship. Her beautiful silk wedding gown, traditionally
white, was strapless, the bodice encrusted with crystals
and tiny faux pearls, the silk endowed with a wonderful
luminescence. The style, cut by a master, suited her petite
figure perfectly. The skirt flared just enough from a tiny
waist so as not to overwhelm her. There was a short train
at the back. The lustrous fabric of the billowing skirt had
been intricately woven with silver thread that formed a

pattern of roses; tightly closed buds, half open buds, roses in full bloom, all in perfect botanical detail.

It was gorgeous!

Miranda had chosen the rose as the symbol of her wedding. It was a tribute to Kathryn Rylance, her beloved Corin and Zara's late mother. The gesture was said to have reduced Zara to tears. A full circle of white silk roses held the bride's short sunburst tulle veil in place. Around her throat was a necklet of Paspaley South Sea pearls, an incredibly beautiful offering from her adoring groom. Diamond and pearl earrings dropped from her ears, the pearls swinging gently with every movement.

All four bridesmaids were tall and very slim. They dared not be anything else with their closely fitting silk gowns. All wore their hair long, flowing over their shoulders. The bodice of the one-shouldered form-fitting gown was caught by a sparkling jewelled strap. A half-moon of silk roses scattered with Swarovski crystals to represent dew drops was tucked at the most flattering angle behind the ear. As headpieces, they were very beautiful, very flattering, the colour matched to their gowns, which were, in turn, the *exact* shade of the bride's favourite roses from the garden, all of them prize blooms.

Zara, the chief bridesmaid, wore a glorious deep *Peace* pink. The shade acted as a wonderful foil for the second bridemaid's lovely lavender-pink gown. Shimmering sunshine-yellow was chosen for the third dark-haired bridesmaid and, on the bride's blonde cousin, the beautiful soft apricot of the old-fashioned musk rose. Miranda and Zara had spent a lot of time poring over fabrics before selecting the luminous silks in precisely complementary shades. The outcome was a triumph. Bride and all four of her bridesmaids moved as if bathed in pools of light.

The luxurious bouquets were composed of roses with a fine tracery of green. In themselves, works of art and, again, the bride's favourites, large fragrant garden roses with their buds—not the hothouse variety. Afterwards, a great deal was spoken about the beauty and success of the bride's and her bridesmaids' outfits and truly lovely bouquets, but the groom and his attendants certainly didn't miss out. It had to be accepted that the wonderfully handsome groom was now taken, the other guys were very attractive, but what about the best man? Brooding good looks like that and those blue eyes could drive a girl beserk! At least that was the general opinion.

It was obvious to all that Garrick Rylance was going to be targeted at the reception by all those young women, already fuzzy with emotion, who dared to dream the dream. Fortune was known to favour the daring. Clearly, he would be able to take his pick.

"Let the battle for the attention of the Cattle Baron begin!" one society matron whispered waggishly to another. *"I've never seen a sexier action man in my life!"*

"And not a thing you can do about it, darling!" whispered the other, who just happened to be her sister-in-law.

"Nothing wrong with looking, even for a grandmother!" was the swift retort. *"There's the hero of any girl's dreams! Bit on the dangerous side, maybe!"*

Guests were ferried from the picturesque church, which had been packed to overflowing, to the sumptuous reception in the Rylance mansion's luxuriant gardens. Zara felt so tremulous, her inner voice had recourse to speak sternly to her.

*You can't allow your emotions to overcome you.
Breathe deeply. Restore your calm.*

Not so easy when what she had witnessed was the union
of soulmates. Her heart was filled with happiness for her
brother and for Miranda, her new sister-in-law—sister.
Of course it was. But there was emotional upheaval as
well. Only once during the ceremony had Garrick's gaze
locked with hers. Just the space of a few searing seconds,
both of them standing immobile. The brilliant blue of his
eyes, bluer than the deep vibrant blue of the sky, seemed
to be mocking her. She had been the first to look away.
It was as if he was telling her she had let her only chance
of real happiness slip away from her.

Ah, the piercing ache of loss!

She couldn't allow it to claw at her heart. Not today.
Today was one of celebration. She was the chief bridesmaid. She had an important role to play. Feeling as she
did, Zara would have been surprised to learn she looked
the very picture of beauty and serenity, her great dark eyes
eloquent with the love and happiness she felt for the bridal
couple. Her family. As chief bridesmaid, she sat to Corin's
right. Garrick, as best man, was seated beside Miranda, so
they were a good few feet apart. The other bridesmaids
and the groomsmen alternated down the long rectangular
bridal table, positioned centre front, so all the guests had
a clear view of them. Exquisite garlands of gilded organza
and chenille roses ran the perimeter of the table, framing
it, with strands of gold beads and faux white pearls that
had an amazing sheen. The bride and her bridesmaids
had used their lovely bouquets to deck the table instead
of arrangements.

The food was sumptuous; the drink the finest vintage
champagne. Corin offered a deeply touching speech to his
bride that moved many to tears. Garrick's speech created

a fine balance. A moment or two of high seriousness, as was to be expected, then his speech moved to the entertaining, with highlights from his and Corin's boyhood. In particular an incident when they were ten, when he had talked Corin into an adventure; catapulting themselves out into the river by means of a stout rope, he had slung from one of the overhanging trees. It wouldn't have been so bad, only the river was running a thrilling white foaming banker at the time.

"An Outback kid, you see," he explained, to indulgent general laughter.

Bring on the Outback, sighed every last female.

"We both lived to tell the tale." A flashing grin from Corin. Both of them had gotten into a lot of trouble. Garrick was a *"wild bush boy, as headlong as a brumby"* his father had thundered, all the more furious because Garrick wasn't flustered or fearful. In fact, Garrick had been remarkably cool for a ten-year-old kid.

Zara remembered too. Their mother had been perturbed—the river, after all, was deep and swift, and in flood—but she had withheld any show of anger. Both boys were excellent swimmers but her father had gone to town, dressing them down for the recklessness of their actions. Garrick had told him repeatedly that he was the instigator, but to no avail. Garrick had looked suitably chastised, but no way had he been in awe of her father and his lashing tongue. Even then, her heart had been stirred by admiration. Perhaps her father had decided that very day that Garrick would forever be on the outer. Dalton Rylance had been so used to people kowtowing to him he would accept nothing less.

At last it was time for the married couple to leave. They were spending a night in Sydney. From there they would fly to Los Angeles, stay a week or so on the West

Coast, then fly to New York. To much excitement, waving arms, a little light shoving and non-stop pleas to "throw it to me!" Miranda let her exquisite bouquet soar like a bird from the upstairs balcony into the blossoming field of beautifully dressed young women, themselves like flowers.

Zara kept her hands down and her eyes lowered. The man she yearned for, now standing only a few feet away, was laughing at the antics of one of the bridesmaids who, right from the wedding rehearsal, had made no secret of the fact that she found the best man "absolutely gorgeous—a guy a girl would follow anywhere!"

She, on the other hand, had played her part as chief bridesmaid with grace and dignity, but in no way did she lose her head, even slightly, or her sense of occasion. After the Hartmann affair, when she had been so falsely accused of being, at best, his mistress, at worst, privy to his business dealings, she had felt like a woman who lived in a house with glass walls. Those who had wanted to for a variety of reasons, mostly because she was an heiress— *rolling in money*—threw rocks.

She had told herself a thousand times she was too sensitive for her own good. She was so much like her mother and what had happened to her mother was a great weight on her shoulders. Some women were more vulnerable than others.

Like a bird on guided wings, Miranda's bouquet, aimed at Zara, landed with a burst of fragrance against Zara's breast. There were groans of disappointment, many more congratulatory cheers. There was great goodwill towards Zara within the extended family and beyond. Zara was so beautiful yet so modest, with the sweetest possible nature. Just like her late mother, Kathryn, beloved of them all and sadly missed.

"You're next, Zara!" a soft voice fluted in her ear. Chloe, one of her young cousins.

Her grandmother, Sibella De Lacey, looking stunning in royal blue silk with a striking broad-brimmed hat, came up to her, taking her arm. "Is this a happy omen, my darling?" she whispered, full of protective love for her granddaughter.

"Nan, Miri aimed this at me deliberately," Zara said wryly.

"And she's a darn good shot." Sibella laughed. "What you have to do now, my darling, is put your life in order. There's a whole *new* life, a whole way of being, open to you. As a Christian, I should say God rest his soul, but your father had a lot to answer for. He failed you on so many levels."

Zara knew the ocean of tears her grandmother had wept for her mother. No easy way out of grief. Sometimes no way at all. "You can't forgive him, can you?"

"No, I can't," Sibella bluntly confessed. "Not for my Kathryn. Not for all eternity. And for shutting you out. When you appeared to have found happiness, he decided to inflict more suffering. He banished the young Garrick from your life. Such an intensely ambivalent man, your father. He really did love your mother in those early years but, gentle though she was, Kathryn refused to fit the mould. The *other one* did that."

"She took great care to do it," Zara said.

"Of course. Leila was prepared to do anything to get Dalton. Afterwards, I believe Dalton came to hate himself. He couldn't look back on what he'd done. How Leila came to have that very special child, one would never know."

"Good grandparents, Nan!" Zara said. "They would have been lovely people. Leila was a one-off."

"Dazzling, yet nothing to her!" Sibella said sardonically.

"She did everything in her power to sideline you. Jealousy. So much like your mother, you see. This may not have been obvious to you, my darling, but Dalton had a powerful jealousy of Garrick."

Zara looked at her grandmother in astonishment. "Garrick? Don't you mean Corin? Dad's dominant characteristic was keeping control."

"Bullying, don't you mean?" Sibella said. "Splitting you and Garrick up was your father's revenge. In no way was Garrick the kind of son-in-law he had in mind. He wanted a *yes, sir, no sir* man, someone who would conform. Someone he could take into the business so he'd have you both beneath his eye and under his control. He could never do that with Garrick. What did Dalton call him again?' She sought Zara's dark eyes. Eyes that Kathryn, then Zara had inherited from her.

Zara had to smile. "The *wild bush boy!* Garrick never went in awe of Dad. His attitude was even more pronounced than Corin's. Even as a boy of ten, Garrick was a man in the making. I turned out a real wimp by comparison. Dad's domination of me should have ended with my adolescence, Nan. I should have been strong enough to break free. Why wasn't I?" she agonized.

"I'll tell you why!" Sibella had to hold down her wrath. "We're talking about a tyrannical man here. Control was a compulsion. Here was a man who made tough competitors crack. It would have been easy to strip my daughter of all her confidence. She should never have married him, but she wanted him at the time. He was very cunning, determined to win her, whatever the cost. Kathryn, as a girl and a young woman, had a wonderful inner contentment and her own strength. That was the sad part. Yet, within a few years, your father had drained it. Stripped her of her happiness. You children were everything to her."

Zara felt such a wave of pain that she hid her face in Miranda's fragrant bouquet. "Dad robbed me of my confidence as well. He pretended—he was *so* convincing and I was thrilled he was even paying me attention—he was acting in my best interests. He convinced me no way would I fit into Garrick's way of life. He told me I simply wouldn't be able to handle any future role as Garrick's wife and mistress of Cooranga. He pointed out to me that Mummy had felt pushed to the limit, having to assume the role of wife and partner of an important industrialist like himself. That's what was responsible for the breakdown in the marriage, he said."

"*Not* Leila, then," Sibella commented bitterly. "Dalton was in all areas of his life a control freak."

"He couldn't control Corin."

Sibella nodded with understanding and pride. "Not my Corin. But don't forget, my darling, there was a marked contrast in how Dalton treated Corin and how he treated you, his only daughter. You were too young to lose your mother. Kathryn acted as the buffer between you children and your father. You in particular because you shared her gentle nature. She angled herself between you and Dalton. We lost her, Zara, but she never *meant* it She would never have deliberately left you."

"No!" Zara nodded when she didn't really know at all. Some questions would forever remain unanswered. But no way was she going to add to her grandmother's grief.

Sibella spoke very quietly. "She's here today, you know."

"I've felt her," Zara said in an equally quiet voice. "Corin told me he did too."

"Every day of my life I pray for her and for you, Zara. You are so much like Kathryn, it's as though she's still with us. Now, I want you to do something for me. Garrick is standing only a few feet away. The two of us are going to stroll over for a chat. Garrick and I always did get on well. He might be smiling at that very frisky girl in the lovely blue dress, but I know where his thoughts are. You must try for a reconciliation, Zara. Too many years have been wasted."

Beneath the silk of her beautiful bridesmaid's dress, her heartbeat was urgent. "I've told you, Nan. He hates me." Her grandmother had long since pried out of her her short-lived love affair with Garrick and its disastrous end.

"Garrick is a proud man." Sibella glanced once more in Garrick's direction. Garrick Rylance, so tall, bold, bronzed, vividly handsome! He could not have been more striking. His brilliant blue eyes framed by thick sooty lashes any girl would die for. A challenging man was Garrick. Never a devil like her late son-in-law, Dalton. "Garrick has it firmly in his head you threw him over, no matter how often you tried to explain. But I've caught him watching you. Garrick might still be angry with you, my darling, but *hate* you? Never! Neither of you has settled for anyone else, I notice, when both of you could have just about anyone. I find that very telling, don't you?"

Garrick knew Zara and her grandmother were coming his way. There had scarcely been a second when he hadn't been aware of Zara, despite the audacious attentions of several young women so hell-bent on flirtation one would have thought their lives depended on it. The one he was with now fitted the bill. She was a real stayer. The sad thing was, he only had eyes for Zara. That was his bitter fate. Being anywhere near her was like being electrified. She looked so beautiful in that pink silk gown, her long dark hair falling like a bolt of shining silk down her back.

He loved the exquisite pink roses that dipped in under her ear. It had been a monumental effort trying to keep his eyes off her.

You're totally messed up, Rylance. He'd told himself that repeatedly. Didn't do much good. His feelings for Zara would never die. They wouldn't even die down and it was years later. Maybe he ought to arrange a session with a really good shrink, he thought with a flash of humour.

How to cure obsession—for one particular woman.

He had already spoken to Sibella, of course. He greatly admired her. Zara was very much like her in appearance. Sibella De Lacey, nearing seventy, remained a beautiful woman. She looked after herself and dressed superbly, no doubt aided by the fact that she had retained her slender figure. He knew Sibella liked him. He knew that if Sibella could wave her magic wand she would make everything come right between himself and Zara. That was if Sibella could ever find her lost magic wand.

Zara, still holding Miranda's lovely bouquet like some magic charm, drew a deep breath. Said a silent prayer. Perhaps she and Garrick could never get back to what they had had, but she had to try.

Her time was running out.

Celebrations continued on into the night, with couples dancing on the rear terrace to a great band who were enjoying themselves as much as anyone else. Others roamed the extensive gardens, which were lit by thousands and thousands of white fairy lights that decked the trees. Flirtations aplenty were going on. A lot of tender hand-holding. Delectable kisses stolen in the scented semi-dark. One overeager, overenthusiastic young male guest for a bit of fun launched himself into the swimming pool with its flotilla of big beautiful hibiscus blooms, but further silliness on the part of others was swiftly discouraged by an unobtrusive security man, dressed like the other guests, who hauled him out.

Older guests retired to the house, agog at the wonderful renovations. They flowed through the main reception rooms and the library, chattering and exclaiming, coming to settle into the opulent sofas and armchairs to go over the great day in detail and catch up on all the latest news and gossip. Many who had thought of her often that day went to gaze with a moment's sadness at the life-size portrait of Kathryn Rylance. It hadn't been seen for quite a while. Certainly not during the reign of the second wife, Leila. Recently it had been taken out of storage, cleaned, reframed and it now hung above the splendid white marble fireplace.

"In its rightful place!" murmured one of Kathryn's friends to another.

Kathryn Rylance had been such a beautiful gracious woman! How sad that she couldn't have been here on this day of days, the wedding of her only son. All agreed that Zara was the image of her, both in looks and in manner. All had decided Miranda had deliberately thrown her bouquet to her sister-in-law. Didn't that declare to the whole world that the two young women were very close? No one had seen such happiness in the Rylance household for far too long.

The King is dead. Long live the King!

By one o'clock in the morning the last of the guests departed in chauffeured limousines that stood waiting for them. This service had been planned well in advance, the thinking being that, very few would be in any condition to drive their own cars. One woman guest was so grateful and maybe so tipsy she started to cry.

"How enormously thoughtful!" she gushed as the chauffeur opened the door for her and her husband.

Her husband, an eminent barrister, agreed. "We'd never get home otherwise, my dear."

"God bless you, Corin, old son!" another male guest yelled at the top of his voice amid more cheering. "This entire day has been *perfect*!"

Everyone knew a love match when they saw one. It was enough to make you bawl your eyes out with joy!

At long, long last the house was empty. The army of caterers had attended to every last detail of the clean up before packing their things and leaving. Corin's housekeeper and the major domo, Hannah and Gil McBride, a very efficient couple in their late forties, taken on by Corin, had retired to their own secluded quarters perhaps an hour ago. Their comfortable bungalow was set in the grounds screened by a grove of luxuriant golden canes and only a short walk to the main house by way of an adjoining covered path.

Zara now felt free to roam.

Garrick had gone on with a party of revellers who obviously had no intention of allowing the night to end. She had no idea when and *if* he would be back but if he did he knew how to handle the state-of-the-art security system. Lord knew he'd made a huge impression on a number of young women looking for a rich handsome husband. The one in the beautiful blue dress came to mind—Lisa something. She had overheard Lisa telling a highly interested friend, "Garrick is simply gorgeous! He makes me go weak at the knees!"

She wasn't the only one.

Include yourself!

* * *

Silently, Zara wandered in and out of the huge reception rooms, pausing to admire all over again the glorious flower arrangements. It was she who had suggested the florist to Miranda. Wayne was acknowledged as one of the country's most creative florists and one of the most expensive by a country mile. Wayne had supplied all the flowers for the wedding, the exquisite bouquets for bride and bridesmaids, church, reception and the house. The effects were stunning. No expense had been spared. He could possibly retire if he so chose.

Someone once said the scent of a flower was its soul. She stooped to inhale the intoxicating sweetness of masses and masses of white gardenias arranged in a very tall *famille verte* Chinese vase with long trailing sprays of jasmine. The whole arrangement was supported by fig branches with their green fruit. She remembered her mother had often used this particular vase for her arrangements. Out of nowhere, she was assailed by the vision and, strangely, the unmistakable perfume of pink frangipani branches. Her mother had liked to mix them in with pink or red azaleas. She retained a little snapshot of her childhood—she and her mother picking armloads from the garden, the two of them so happy, so much the loving mother and daughter. No one should have to lose their mother. It was an awful business. She had mourned her father and, to a degree, Leila. Death required attention. But in no way had their deaths caused the enormous grief and feeling of utter loss she had suffered when she and Corin had lost their mother. Neither her father nor Leila had had room in their lives for her.

Tears pricked her eyes. One of the first things Corin had done after the death of their father was to go in search of their mother's portrait. It had been painted by a famous Italian artist, commissioned by their father not long after the marriage. Their father had had it taken down within days of her death. She remembered with a feeling of pride that she had found the courage to volubly protest, Corin even more stridently. The two of them had all but yelled at their domineering, autocratic father. To no avail. Neither of them had had any idea where the painting had been stored. Not in the house. They had looked, risking severe discipline. Corin had finally located the painting in an art dealer's storeroom.

"You're so very beautiful, Mummy," she whispered, looking up at the bravura portrait of her mother in her wedding gown. The irony of it—her wedding gown! "I'm sure you were here today. I *felt* you. So did Corin. So did Nan. We love you so much."

For the first time she spotted a single white rose of exquisite form and fragrance tied with a silver ribbon. It lay on the white marble mantelpiece at the base of the portrait. She picked it up, curious to know who had put it there.

The tiny silver and white card said simply: *From Miranda.*

That a gesture could be so perfect!

Still holding the white rose, she went about quietly turning off banks of switches that controlled the lighting. She would take the rose upstairs with her. Pop it in a bud vase and keep it beside her bed. It was all so extraordinary when one thought about it. Lovely little Miranda, with her essential goodness and brightness, was *Leila's* daughter. Hard to realise, given Leila's cold, calculating, self-absorbed nature. The connection had not come out—Corin had made sure of that. Not that it was the worst story in the world, but it was somewhat bizarre. No one had commented on the fact that Miranda had been given away by her New Zealand grandfather, a distinguished professor of medicine. Nor that a New Zealand cousin had made a beautiful bridesmaid. Maybe someone would uncover the true story as the years passed. It would make no difference to Corin and Miranda. Nor to her and her grandparents. Garrick was the only one who had raised a question about what appeared to have gone over everyone else's head. But Garrick didn't *know*.

Radiant moonlight was coming in through the many tall windows and the side lights of the front door. She could easily see her way across the entrance hall. She planned to leave a few lights on for Garrick, anyway. He had such a powerful effect on women. Always had, even if he had been genuinely unaware of it. Yet the highly eligible Garrick seemed no more successful at putting back the pieces than she was. The one had altered the life of the other.

She felt anger rising in her at her father's multiple deceptions. The way he had worked on her to strip her of all confidence. Her father, therefore, had been her enemy. Good fathers affirmed their children's value. She had received no such validation from him. She had to accept, too, that somewhere along the line Garrick must have become a point of bitter antagonism. When one considered it, her father had shown all the signs of pathological jealousy. Business giant or not, Dalton Rylance had been a very strange man.

She had only walked a few feet towards the grand staircase when the front door suddenly opened. It *had* to be Garrick. She spun just in time to see his tall, muscular figure outlined against the exterior lights.

"Garrick!" She felt the breathless vibrations of her heart.

"Well, what do we have here," he mocked, "a welcoming

party of one?" He slowly approached, devastatingly hand-some in his formal pearl-grey morning suit. He hadn't bothered to change. That would have been an additional excitement for the young women in his party.

His tone was so sardonic she waved the taunt away with her hand. "Have no fear. I didn't think you'd even come back. You seemed to be getting along so well with…Lisa, wasn't it?"

"Louise," he said with a drawl. "Call me Lou!"

"Well, I was close." She shrugged, the jewelled strap that held the one-shouldered bodice of her gown giving off sparkles of light. "Didn't work out?"

"*I* prefer to do the chasing," he said, turning back to reactivate the alarm system. Then he recommenced his graceful walk, sleek as a panther, across the expanse of black and white marble tiles. "Still wearing your brides-maid gown?" There was an oddly seductive note in his voice, given he had done his level best to avoid her the entire evening. One more or less obligatory dance, both of them remaining silent, their bodies locked in tension, the two of them divided even when his arm was tight around her.

"I haven't been upstairs yet." The raggedness of her breath betrayed her. "I'm not in the least tired."

"You should never take that dress off." He didn't sound as much admiring as maddened by how she looked. Her small perfect breasts were outlined against the luminous silk. "Why is it you're so extravagantly beautiful, Zara?" It came out like an unrelenting lament. "Why is it a part of me still madly wants you? God, sometimes I think you nailed me when we were only kids. Zara, the little princess! I'd never seen such a beautiful little girl before or since."

Her limbs felt heavy, as though heat was bearing down

on her. She turned fully to confront him. "Drink has loosened your tongue, Garrick."

"Maybe it has," he admitted with a wry laugh, moving ever closer. "How come you got over me just like that—" his fingers clicked "—when I can't seem to put you behind me?"

She managed a sceptical laugh, tilting her chin. "You're just wound up."

And you aren't?

"You *did* put me behind you, Garrick," she said. "Very successfully, I would say."

"A matter of opinion, my dear," he drawled. "*I'd* say not terribly well. More's the pity! What have you got in your hand?"

She held the white rose up to the shimmering moonlight. "A beautiful little gesture from Miranda. She left it in front of my mother's portrait."

"How very sweet!" He smiled, sounding unsurprised. "Corin is a lucky man. Miranda has my full approval. *I'd* like to drink a toast to your mother, Zara. I had the feeling she was here today—in spirit, anyway. I didn't see as much of her as I would have liked, but I remember her as the loveliest woman. She was so kind to me when your father lived to bawl me out. I remember my mother receiving the news of her death with tears rolling down her cheeks. She doesn't cry easily; she's learned to hide her tears."

"Some of us have to," Zara pointed out quietly.

"Did you cry for me?"

She couldn't bear the hurtful edge to his voice. "A million times!"

"Liar!" He shook his handsome dark head. "Just a mad fling, wasn't it?"

"It was *mad*, certainly!" The most exultant experience

she had ever had. There was all the difference in the world between being passionately in love and giving and receiving the loving affection that brought a lot of people to marriage. So many degrees of loving! Piled one upon another.

"Well, you got over it soon enough." In the intimate semi-darkness he reached for her. "Come with me."

Her legs felt like those of a newborn foal, barely able to support her. Every time he looked at her she remembered the rapture, then the heartbreak. Unsurprisingly, she lost her composure. Emotion *could* be uncontrollable. At least that was her experience with Garrick. "What is it you *want*, Garrick?" she asked in a soft ragged voice. "You want to see me cry?"

"Zara, *darling*, I have seen you cry, remember?" His answer was sardonic. "All crocodile tears." He drew her into the opulent living room, switching lights back on as they went.

"Why did you never answer my letters?" Her accusation flew at him. Her voice sounded the old heartbreak. Yet he made no response. She dragged back against his strong hand. "Answer me, you ghastly, ghastly man!"

At that, he jerked them both to such an abrupt halt that her body slammed into his. "Do you understand nothing?" he asked harshly. "*Sweetheart*, I never read any of them."

She had always held on to the hope that he had at least read some of them. Now she felt shattered. She had poured out her heart in those letters, telling him of her hatred for herself for being such a fool as to be so effortlessly manipulated by her father. "But I sent you so many!" Her expression was eloquent with pain. "God, *how* many? You never read *any* of them. You *can't* be telling the truth!"

"Even more serious than that, Zara, my lost love; I

burnt the lot of them." There was a bitter twist to his beautifully shaped sensuous mouth. "Had a little bonfire. You made it very plain you were done with me, remember? You revealed yourself for what you were. Probably still are. A woman who has the power to bring a man to his knees. Were you planning on keeping the torture going? Now that's sick! I wasn't having any. I have my pride. You ought to consider you're more like your father than you think."

"What?" She reacted with horror, stunned that he should say such a thing. Indeed, her shock was so great that the air turned red before her eyes. Anti-violence all her life, without a second's thought, she brought up her hand and struck him as hard as she possibly could across the face. He could easily have stopped her by grasping her wrist, his reflexes were such. But for some reason, he didn't. He took the blow. "I'm *nothing* like my father," she said very tightly. "He was a cruel, cruel man."

"You'll get no argument from me." His answer was as dry as ash. "You took a chance hitting out at me, Zara." As he spoke, he was making a production out of rubbing his cheekbone. His skin was so tanned the red imprint of her fingers barely showed. "I could have retaliated."

"I'm sorry," she said, when she wasn't at all ashamed of her actions. He deserved it. There was immense pleasure in connecting, if only in a blow.

"No, you're not," he bluntly contradicted. "You *loved* it!"

"I did!" She admitted to it in a low voice, moving closer and staring into his burning blue eyes.

"Course you did!" he taunted. "So…I'd say what's good for the goose is good for the gander."

Tears of rage filled her eyes but he grabbed her, hauling her into his arms. How many times had he wanted to do that since he'd arrived? It was perilous being around Zara. She could have resisted, but she made no movement to draw back. "Hartmann a good lover?" With an effort, he kept his tone purely conversational.

Diamond pinpoints of light stood in her desperate eyes. He pulled her ever closer. "Did he tell you you have the most beautiful, the most kissable mouth in the world? Don't bother struggling. You won't get away." He held her strongly with his left hand, brought up his right to touch her long hair, tipping her face up to his. "Be careful now how you answer," he warned.

Anger burned past raw pain. "He did. He *did!*" She laughed in his face, her own face pale. "Of course he d—" She got no further.

He was under too much strain. Cursing her. Cursing himself. There was no reprieve with Zara.

He opened his mouth wide over hers, claiming it completely, sick to death with wanting her. It was a brutal kind of rapture to be with her, to have her captive in his arms, to kiss her again after such an eternity. The fire would never burn out. He had to believe she was feeling the heat too because her whole body was undulating, as though her tender woman's flesh was melting at his touch.

Once she tried to draw back, making a sound of dissent as if she were in a rage. But he knew it for what it was. No more than excited defiance. He *knew*. He definitely knew. She could no more subdue the powerful sexual flame that sprang fiercely between them than he could—a flame that had been ignited years before. He wasn't going to listen to any play acting. He'd had more than enough of that. He plunged his fingers into her long heavy hair, keeping her face up to him.

"Damn, damn, damn you, Garrick!" she cried, as though her emotions were too powerful to be contained.

"Sounds more like praying to me," he taunted. "Anyway, I've damned *you* a thousand times." His tongue worked over and around her closed lips, increasing the pressure, prising them apart. It had to be driving her crazy because her mouth opened fully and her breath mingled with his.

Paradise regained.

He was kissing her the way he wanted to kiss her. The way he kissed her in his dreams. Not tenderly, but a furious combative passion that demanded release. Sensation swirled all around them. Images of them together filled his mind. Now and in the past. He had her back where she belonged. In his arms. He couldn't seem to care about all the rest. Her flight from Coorango. The betrayal he'd felt. He had her with him right now. He wasn't going to let her go.

Not tonight. He hadn't planned it. How so? When he knew it was going to take place.

Zara had a fear she might faint. So much pressure was building in her. In her back, in her stomach, her breasts and her legs. Her body swayed against his, her aching breasts pressed hard against the muscular plane of his chest. She hungered for him so much she was shaking uncontrollably. The strength of his hold on her increased. It came to her belatedly that he was supporting her. The rose had slipped out of her fingers. It was crushed somewhere between them. Its sweet fragrance was scenting the air. She felt trapped. At the same time she felt she was where she belonged.

"I could have picked any other girl in the world," he muttered, his lips against her throat, "but it had to be *you*! So let's choose a bed," he said with a shuddering laugh. "Yours or mine?" He raised his hand, clasping her neck beneath the heavy fall of her hair.

"Don't sound so cynical, Garrick," she begged, her voice a jagged whisper.

"Ah, be damned to everything!" he cried, as though the situation was utterly intolerable. He caught her chin, turned her face up to him. "You *can't* be crying?" he rasped.

A single tear had escaped, edging down her cheek.

"Do you think your tears make me fair game?" His expression carried no gentleness whatever. It showed tension as tight as a piano wire strung to perfect pitch.

"It's always about *you,* isn't it?" she lashed back. "You and your abominable pride! Well, it cost us." She closed her eyes against him, realizing he would never forgive her until the day he died. Her heart was drumming in her ears, the beat strong enough to make her deaf. A great flush of sexual excitement was covering her body in a tide. She thought of a dam, its massive walls giving way.

"Drop the tears, Zara," he advised. "They won't work. Tonight you're *mine*. It will be just like old times!" He put one steely muscled arm beneath her and then swept her off her swooning feet.

There were no words in her mind to stop him. She knew it would happen. They both knew it would happen. Both of them wanted the torture over. If only for a single night. She needed no man in her life. Unless it was Garrick. He needed no woman. Unless it was *her*. Both of them were in the fierce grip of obsession. A maelstrom of passion that had at its core a fatal flaw.

There could be no real love, no real future without *trust*.

She could never hope to make him trust her again. He had not even read *one* of her letters. The pain of it seared her so badly she doubted she would ever mention those letters again. Her father was dead. She couldn't confront him, make him confess to Garrick what he had said and done to drive them apart.

All she knew was that it was her lot to love Garrick. Every which way. No matter what happened. Until death did them part.

CHAPTER FOUR

THEY flew into Coorango at noon on a blazing blue day. It had been a smooth flight, now they were taxiing into the massive silver hangar that housed the Beech Baron and a metallic blue Eurocopter with a broad white stripe. This had to be the latest addition to the fleet, Zara thought. She was familiar with this particular luxury helicopter. Her father, now Corin, retained one for private use. Two other helicopters, chartered aircraft, sat like fat yellow birds just off the concrete apron. Aerial mustering was obviously in progress.

Coming in over the airstrip, she could see Garrick's mother, Helen, was on hand to greet them. Helen was standing with her back against a four-wheel drive, no doubt to ferry them up to the homestead. She had started waving minutes before they touched down. Zara waved back, appreciative of the fact that Helen had made the effort to come down herself. She could easily have sent someone. It made her feel very welcome. She hoped Garrick's father, Daniel—lovely man—was having a good day. She knew he lived his life in constant pain, but dealt with it without complaint. Apparently his response to all enquiries regarding his state of health was "getting there!" Garrick had told her rather tensely that his father's health was a source of great concern to his mother, to him and his sister Julianne, and everyone who knew and loved Daniel Rylance. This was a man greatly respected in the Outback.

Zara found herself wishing for the umpteenth time that her own father had been such a man. How different life might have been! Her beautiful loving mother might still be with them. Her own love affair with Garrick would never have been so brutally severed. She had blamed herself for years for the way things had turned out. But Garrick's behaviour, she now realized, hadn't helped. There was anger as well as sadness in that. She could barely take it in that he hadn't read her letters. If he *had*, the ongoing pain and estrangement might well have been settled. How lives could be messed up through a lack of communication, she thought. It must happen all the time. People keeping silent when they should speak out. And, as a result, one could be faced with a lifetime of regrets.

"Zara, dear, you have no idea how good it is to see you again!" Helen Rylance, looking amazingly youthful in yellow cotton jeans and a white tank top, her arms wide and embracing, greeted the young woman who was everything she could want in a daughter-in-law.

It had really upset her and Daniel when Zara and Garrick's blossoming relationship had abruptly foundered. Although nothing had been said, one would have had to be blindfolded not to recognize how passionately in love they had fallen. Yet it was all over—just like that! And no credible explanations either. In time Garrick had become engaged to Sally Forbes, a confident young woman known to them from childhood. They would have settled for Sally, only she and Daniel just *knew* where their son's heart lay. Helen also knew intuitively that Dalton Rylance, the master manipulator, had brought about the end of that blossoming relationship.

It had struck her forcibly as revenge—on her. Dalton had disliked her intensely, thought her far too opinionated. A woman wasn't allowed an opinion contrary to his own. Revenge on Garrick, as her son. Lord knew she had never made any big secret of her wariness where Dalton Rylance was concerned. He had been such a bully! Her dislike and distrust had been well and truly out in the open after Kathryn's tragic early death. She couldn't think of that terrible event without a tear escaping. Such a lovely woman Kathryn had been. Zara was the image of her. The resemblance, both in looks and manner, would have added to Dalton's ferocious guilt. Ruthless billionaire he might have been, an acknowledged captain of industry, but he had been a shocking failure on the home front. A man of notorious temper, he had killed the gentle, sensitive Kathryn's spirit with his dominance, his aggression and push for total control. He had deliberately set about masterminding his daughter's life.

Now he was dead and Zara was no longer forced to walk in his shadow. That business with the Hartmann character must have caused Zara endless problems. There were inherent dangers in being a very beautiful, highly desirable woman. No doubt Hartmann had wanted to add Zara to his collection. Zara had from the beginning denied any close relationship. Those who knew Zara believed her. Hartmann had been exposed for what he was—a white-collar criminal who wasn't quite as clever as he thought.

* * *

"I'll drive, Ellie," Garrick said to his mother without pre-amble. "You sit in the back with Zara."

Helen handed over the keys. She had instantly intuited that her son and Zara had picked up on their complex relationship. It sizzled in the air around them. But re-suming their relationship didn't automatically heal all the wounds of the past. She had been shocked when Garrick, only recently, had reluctantly come out with the dread-fully dismaying news that he had burned all of Zara's letters. *Unread!* As a woman, she had sided with Zara and her feelings. One way or another, her proud son hadn't given Zara a chance to explain herself and her actions. No wonder there were a whole lot of conflicting emotions there. She prayed that Zara's stay on Coorango would finally uncover the truth. She wasn't such a fool that she didn't know Zara still deeply cared for her son. Even the way she looked at him shouted that fact to his mother, if not to him.

Ah, well, one could only hope that the peace and free-dom of Coorango would work its magic. There was a rush now for her beloved Daniel to see his only son settled, if not actually married, before he went. In the book of life her beloved husband's had reached the final chapter. His medical reports didn't get any better. The prognosis wors-ened as his medication got stronger. How she was going to live without him, she couldn't yet face. At any rate, Zara was here—she and Daniel had conspired to invite her without telling their son—their goal being to reunite these two young people they considered perfect for one another. Dalton Rylance had been the one responsible for the huge shift in direction. The invitation to Coorango was to make up for lost time.

* * *

Zara rolled down the window so she could inhale the wonderfully aromatic smells of the bush. There was the king of trees, the ubiquitous gum yielding several valuable oils, as well as honey and prolific quantities of blossom in glorious colours. The wildflowers, the native boronia, the scented water lilies which floated like cargo on the surface of the innumerable lagoons. She even loved the smell of the baking fiery red earth, the silver haze of the mirage dancing amid the brilliant sunshine.

"Oh, I've missed this!" She gave a deeply voluptuous sigh, eyes shut tight in a kind of bliss, so she was unaware of Garrick's intense gaze in the rear-view mirror.

"It's been far too long, Zara." Helen pressed the young woman's arm. "Welcome back to Coorango. Daniel is so pleased you decided to come."

Up front, Garrick gave a sardonic laugh. "Good of you and Dad to tell me."

"You're supposed to say *thank you*, darling." Helen smiled. "Your father and I wanted to keep it as a big surprise."

"Take my word for it, it *was*," he said very dryly. "You could have knocked me over with a feather."

"At least you got over the shock fairly quickly," Zara offered sweetly and, it had to be said, provocatively.

"Just sparring, Ellie," Garrick told his highly attentive matchmaking mother. "How's Dad today?"

"Really looking forward to seeing you,' Helen said. "I hope you've brought lots of photographs of the wedding along with all the news. You must have made a very beautiful bridesmaid, Zara."

Zara, who wasn't in the least vain, went a little pink. "Not as beautiful as the bride."

"Of course not. That's only to be expected." Helen smiled.

"Looking glorious is nothing new for Zara, Ellie," Garrick said with the faintest edge. Zara was wearing white—a fine cotton sleeveless shirt with white linen trousers. Her dark mane of hair was arranged in a neat coil on her nape. Her beautiful skin looked as cool and matt as a lily. Imagine that—blossoming beneath the hot Outback sun! "Miranda tossed her the bridal bouquet and, though our Zara did her level best to avoid it, it landed right on target in her arms," he told his mother.

Zara met his burning blue eyes. "I didn't think you noticed."

"Oh, I did. There wasn't a guy at the wedding who didn't think you'd make the most glorious catch."

"But you're in the market yourself, my dear," his mother pointed out with more than a touch of mischief.

"Don't start again, Ellie," he warned.

"By the way—" Helen abruptly sobered "—I have some news I'd better get out of the way. Sally and Nick are having problems. Thought I should mention it as they'll be here for the Trophy."

"That's the polo finals?" Zara asked, at the same time registering a zap of unease at Helen's news. The word *ex-fiancée* sprang instantly to mind.

Helen nodded. "This year they're to be held on Coorango." She patted Zara's hand. "You couldn't have come at a better time!"

Garrick cut in crisply. "I'm supposed to believe this about Sally and Nick?"

"Come on, darling," Helen retorted smartly. "I got it right from the horse's mouth. Josephine Forbes doesn't get things wrong. Sally is her daughter after all."

"But that's terrible!" Garrick groaned. He sounded stunned. "I had no idea the marriage was in trouble. I thought they were very happy."

"Not happy enough, apparently." Helen sighed. "You remember Sally, don't you, Zara?"

"Of course I do. I thought her very attractive," she said with genuine warmth. "I'm sorry to hear they're having problems, but I'm sure they can work things out. They haven't been married all that long?"

Helen swallowed the word that had flashed into her head—*rebound*. Sally hadn't given herself enough time to get over Garrick. She'd thought the best way to solve the tough time she was having was to marry Nick, who was one of Garrick's closest friends. "Two years," Helen told Zara rather wryly. "They'll be here for the Trophy next weekend. Thought I'd better let you know sooner rather than later."

"Spared me the trouble of having to find out myself," Garrick said, not bothering to hide his exasperation. "God, poor old Sal!"

"A worrying time for Nick too, dear," Helen pointed out.

"Of course. It wouldn't do a bit of good for us to put ourselves in the middle, Ellie." It sounded very much like a warning. "They have to work it out themselves." He reflected for a moment, his expression serious. "Sal wanted children. Could that be a problem, do you think?"

"Scarcely a problem *yet*, darling," Helen said. "A little suggestion from your mother, though. I wouldn't find myself alone with Sally if I were you."

Garrick pinned his mother's eyes in the rear vision. "For God's sake, Ellie, what is that supposed to mean?"

Helen shook her burnished head. "I don't think you

need delve too deeply, my darling. Anyway, I've told you and that's the end of that!"

Even as she spoke, Helen knew full well it wasn't.

So, incidentally, did Zara. So many lessons in life to learn from! One being—marry in haste, repent at leisure. She sincerely hoped that wasn't going to be the case here. Yet she couldn't help the most awful suspicion.

Zara had heard all the stories about the swashbuckling George William Rylance who had built Coorango Homestead, a twenty-room mansion, in the late eighteen-seventies. The man was a legend, an Outback icon. Such a splendid house—no matter if it was smack bang in the middle of the Never Never—had put the seal of success on the young English adventurer. The seventh son of a baronet, George had accepted a sizeable stake from his father to make his own fortune in the best way he knew how. Shortly after, he and a like-minded cousin had set sail for Australia, where George fully expected to found his own dynasty and make his fortune in some sort of pastoral enterprise. Sheep, perhaps?

After all, it was a British Army officer, John Macarthur, who had laid the foundations for the country's wool industry. It was well established by the time Macarthur died in the mid-eighteen-hundreds and George arrived. George had seen over Camden Park, a very handsome Regency-style mansion dreamed of by Macarthur but built by his sons after his death. He, too, had wanted something as substantial.

The homestead, to the Australian squattocracy, occupied much the same position as an Englishman's castle so George singled out a very fine architect working in South Australia at the time to build him an Outback castle.

Never mind it was on the fringe of the great Australian desert. This area, he'd had the vision to see, was destined to become the home of the nation's cattle kings. George, with all the confidence of a man born to succeed, had already turned his attention to cattle. Becoming a cattle baron—a touch of flamboyancy showed there—suited him much better than farming sheep. Besides, he had become greatly enamoured by the vastness, the extraordinary colourations and the strange and lonely grandeur of the continent's Interior. Here was where he wanted to put down roots. The Rylances were men of the land. Here, in this extraordinary area of ancient flood plains, criss-crossed by a great maze of water channels, creeks and lagoons, he was going to dig in. Just to be on the safe side, he had invested rather heavily in gold, which soon began returning him healthy profits.

It was just over a mile from the airstrip to the home compound. The drive was lined by gigantic date palms, brought in and planted over a century and a half before by Afghan traders.

Presently, the front elevation of Coorango Homestead came into view. To Zara's eye, it clearly revealed the architect's nationality and background, which was Italian. The two-storey building was of grand proportions, but very pleasing. A dynastic *home*, not a fortress. She particularly loved the pinkish-gold sandstone that had been used in its construction. Slender double pillars and wonderfully ornamental white cast iron lace balustrades designed by the architect framed the upper balcony and wrapped around the other three sides of the building. Italian too was the magnificent three-basin stone fountain that featured rearing horses to support the largest bowl.

"It's playing today in your honour." Helen smiled with pleasure at her guest. Zara was *here*. That in itself she considered a coup.

"How lovely!" Zara's voice lilted. She pointed to the plume of water. "Look, it's sending rainbow shot spray over the agapanthus." Masses and masses of the hardy plant, all a deep lavender-blue, encircled the fountain.

Garrick achieved a half wry, half cynical laugh. He knew perfectly well what his mother and father were up to. Matchmaking. Heirs were needed for Coorango. High time he was married. His engagement to Sally had been doomed from the start. But his parents had always been extraordinarily fond of Zara, as they had been of Zara's mother. Ellie had been truly shocked when he'd finally confessed he hadn't read any of Zara's letters.

"But how could you, Garrick?"

He could and he did. His mother hadn't plumbed the depth of his despair. There had been no slow demise of the relationship. It had been short, sharp and brutally final. Dalton Rylance had ruled Zara's life. She had let him. Obviously, she had thought she would never find another man as powerful to measure up. Such a shame Hartmann was such a wicked man!

"And how is Daniel today?" Zara asked, hoping to hear it was one of Daniel's good days.

"So looking forward to seeing you," Helen said. "He has a male nurse these days, Rolf Hammond. He has been a great help. Daniel really likes him. We've sent Rolf off for a short break. You'll meet him when he returns."

Garrick drove slowly around the gravelled drive, naturally for Zara's benefit, bringing the four-wheel drive to a halt at the base of the short flight of stone steps that led to the lower terrace. Its slender columns matched the upper storey but the area had been left open.

Moments later, sunglasses shielding her eyes from the boldest sun imaginable and the bouncing heat, Zara stood out on the drive looking away to left and right. The massive stone walls that bordered the compound and gave it added protection were ablaze with bougainvillea that just had to be *the* plant for the heat and the dry. She realized that what she was looking at were modern hybrids, not the common magenta. Glorious shades of pink, scarlet, crimson, cerise tumbled riotously to the left, white, orange and bronze to the other. The usual flower beds of a more temperate climate were not in evidence. Too hot! But more dense plantings of the indestructible strelizias, the "Bird of Paradise" their wonderful flower heads rising to easily four feet, decorated the wide beds in front of the lower terrace and along the short flight of stone steps.

Helen linked her arm through Zara's, pleased with Zara's unconcealed delight. Zara had always loved Coorango—far more than any city bred girl might have been expected to. Of course Zara painted and extremely well. Her father had ignored her artistic aspirations but she would find plenty of inspiration to paint here. "You'll love what we've done with the gardens at the rear of the house," Helen said with rising enthusiasm. She was so glad to have a woman's company. Life could get lonely. Especially of late as Daniel's cycle of life was coming to an end. "I've long since discovered walled gardens work better here. You'll be amazed at what we've managed to achieve."

"A love of gardens unites people, doesn't it?" Zara answered with a smile. "I'm looking forward to seeing what you've done, Helen. The avenue of date palms is so spectacular. It imparts a wonderful sense of place."

"Well, one must work with the environment. It determines the character of the garden, don't you think?" she asked on a rhetorical note. "So many beautiful flowering plants I've always loved—impossible to grow here, as you can imagine. Now, come along. You must come in too, Rick. Don't race away. Dougal will take care of the luggage."

"A cup of coffee and a sandwich, then I'll be off," Garrick said, reaching into the four-wheel drive for Zara's suitcases. "No need to bother Dougal. This is nothing. Right, Ellie—" he gave the command "—lead the way. There's something I have to discuss with Dad before I go. We need to get rid of O'Donnell. I need to do that right away. Give the man a promotion, an outstation to manage and he spends most of his time drunk."

"You know that for certain, Rick?" Helen frowned. Daniel, not Garrick, had been the one prepared to give O'Donnell the opportunity. It seemed such a shame he had botched it.

"Of course I do," Garrick said with quiet authority. "I'll take the chopper to Biri Biri tomorrow. I'd invite you to come with me, Zara, but I don't want you involved in any unpleasantness. O'Donnell could take dismissal hard."

"Oh, I hope not!" Helen looked anxious.

"No need to worry, Ellie," Garrick said briskly. "I can handle it."

"Sure you can! Garrick can be tougher than anyone in the business when it's necessary," Helen boasted to Zara, not without good reason.

"I'm sure you're right!" Zara gave Garrick a dazzling smile that nevertheless had a bite to it.

"Oh, Zara, it's just so lovely having you here," Helen exclaimed, having missed that exchange. "Anyway, I'm sure Rick has any number of exciting things lined up."

"I'm looking forward to the polo weekend," Zara said, refusing to meet Garrick's sardonic gaze. "Still the big party Saturday night?"

"Of course, my dear,' Helen confirmed happily. "I hope you've brought a pretty dress."

"Zara is not short on those, Mother, dear," Garrick drawled.

At the first sight of Daniel Rylance, sitting in his wheel-chair, Zara had to bite down hard on the inside of her lip so not the faintest cry would escape her. She saw that this fine man was dying. His skin was very pale, dry as parchment, stretched tight as a drum over his once strikingly handsome features. The coal-black hair of yesterday had turned silver-white, as was his neatly clipped beard. Illness had robbed him of his once impressive height, strength and weight. He had lost stones. But his deeply shadowed grey eyes were as penetrating as ever and his smile just as wide. This was a man of great inner strength and courage.

"Zara, my dear, what a treat it is to have you here!" He held up his arms, seeing Kathryn very clearly in her daughter. The same incredibly beautiful dark eyes, so lustrous and full of expression.

"And how good of you to ask me!" Zara moved swiftly across the big beautiful plant-filled room the family had always called the Garden Room. She slipped gracefully to her knees so she could be almost at Daniel's eye level. She took his hands in hers, squeezing them very gently. "And how are you, Daniel? Your eyes are as bright and perceptive as ever!"

"Getting there, Zara," he said with a lopsided grin. "I could do with a kiss on the cheek."

"Kisses on *both* cheeks," she said, rising to her feet. "I'm so happy to be here. I bought you some books I hope you're going to enjoy. The latest from your favourite authors."

She bent to kiss his cheek, right, then left, then right again as he whispered in her ear, "Welcome home, Zara."

Home? She felt a painful wrench of emotion she was just barely able to conceal.

"Maybe you can help Ellie read to me,' Daniel suggested, smiling at his devoted wife. "She's just so good to me. Glued to my side. It isn't fair on her. But I'm having a bit of trouble holding books these days and the medication I'm taking is making my eyesight blurry, so I do enjoy having someone read to me."

"Then Helen and I will work out some shifts," Zara said, waiting on Helen's smiling nod of assent. "Actually, I like the idea. I *love* reading. I'll love reading to *you*."

His father reclined in his wheelchair looking at Zara as if she was an angel sent straight from Heaven, Garrick thought. Both of them wore expressions of great satisfaction.

Daniel looked past Zara to his son, standing there with such eye-catching male grace, so marvellously strong and alive. All he had to do now was survive until Garrick and Zara got back together again. He had no illusions he had much time. "You're going to stay in for lunch, aren't you, Rick?"

"Sure, if you want me to, Dad," Garrick said, although he knew he'd have things to catch up on. Coorango had an excellent foreman, Bill Knox, but Bill tended to get a bit anxious when there were major decisions to be made. Aerial mustering was about to begin and the particular areas of the vast station to be worked needed to be sorted out. He already knew too many of their cattle had strayed over into the desert proper looking for feed. They had to be brought in.

"Of course I want you to! This is a great day," Daniel exclaimed with real enthusiasm. "I haven't felt so well in a long time."

Pray God, the mistakes of the past could be put behind them.

Zara ventured out on her own the following morning. As a horsewoman, she was nowhere in the league of Sally Draper, but she was a lot more accomplished than most city-bred girls. Garrick had flown off to Biri Biri in one of the choppers before she had even had breakfast. But then it was his habit to start the day at sunrise. A typical mustering day, she knew, began well before daybreak. The chartered helicopters had arrived, two of them, because two could cover much more country in less time and control the movement of the cattle so much better.

She was looking forward to watching the muster. She would have to wait until Garrick got back. It was exciting to hear the *whap-whap-whap* of the rotor blades as they sliced through the hot air. Exciting being part of it all. The choppers swept far and wide, pushing small mobs of cattle at a time into the long makeshift "funnels" that led to the holding yards. One of the big holding yards Garrick had had shifted the previous afternoon, telling them over dinner it hadn't been in the right place. Running a cattle station the size of Coorango was a big job for a big man. Garrick had had to take command years before he'd expected to, but he had stepped into his father's shoes with certainty. He had been trained by the best. Operating a vast property was in his blood.

Helen had picked out one of the quieter horses from the stable for her, an exquisitely made little chestnut mare that radiated sweet temper. She was called Satin and Zara could see why. The mare had such an exceptional shiny coat; she might have been groomed for the Melbourne Cup.

"Now, don't go too far, dear," Helen cautioned. "It's quite a while since you've been here."

"Sad to say," Zara commented, stroking the mare's neck. "No further than the Blue Lady Lagoon, Helen, I promise. I'll be home well in time for lunch. Did Garrick say what time he'd be back?"

Helen shook her head. "He'll stay as long as it takes. I'm really disappointed in Patrick. He's been an excellent stockman, but he broke up with his girlfriend in the Alice not all that long ago. Must have been the start of it—the drinking, I mean. We didn't realize she meant all that much to him. He certainly never said. Love affairs that go wrong!" Helen lamented. "They take their toll."

"Know the feeling!" Zara gave the older woman a wry smile.

"*You* are in control of your life now, Zara," Helen said.

As soon as she was out of sight of the main compound and its satellite buildings, Zara gently kicked her heels into the mare's flanks. The response was immediate. Satin was as keen on a gallop as she was. Sweet-tempered she might be, but the mare seemed to revel in the opportunity to put on a show. She surged forward, breaking into a

smooth, long striding gallop that showed her soundness
and quality.

To her added pleasure, a squadron of green and gold
budgerigars, one of the great sights of the Outback, flew
in perfect V formation over their heads, not one breaking
rank. The air vibrated with the pounding of hooves and the
whirr of so many wings. Half a mile from the Blue Lady
Lagoon, she reined into the shade of a large stand of pink
blossoming bauhinias. Fallen petals swirled all around
them like pieces of confetti. She loved the bauhinias, the
orchid trees. They thrived on Coorango.

With a deep sigh of pleasure, she removed her wide
brimmed Akubra, allowing the breeze to cool her face
and neck, then she loosened the bright red bandanna she
wore around her throat for protection. For the ride, she
had fashioned her long hair into a braid that fell down
her back. Only one hitch! The thick braid had given her
back a good thumping while they'd galloped. She took
the opportunity to make a shorter loop of it. Her muscles
were a bit tight, but they would unwind.

She sat quietly, contemplatively in the saddle looking
all around her. Coorango stretched away for ever! Such
savage splendour! It had to be seen to be fully appreciated.
It was, quite simply, awesome. Not a cloud marred the
iridescent perfection of the glittering blue sky, as immense
as the fiery red earth beneath, dotted with the perennial
grass, the spiky Spinifex rings. At this time of year the
prickly mounds were scorched to a dull gold. The heat
of the day was increasing by the minute. She wouldn't
have attempted going any further than the lagoon, anyway.
Best to take things in stages. The mirage was abroad,
that naturally occurring optical phenomenon that could
even be caught on camera. It was so easy to see how the

early explorers had mistaken the desert mirage for bodies
of water. Barely a kilometre away, dozens of little stick
people were running through the silvery layers. Another
familiar illusion.

It was as if she had never been away.

When Garrick landed on Biri Biri Patrick O'Donnell was
nowhere to be found. O'Donnell had two part-Aboriginal
jackeroos to help him. Mustering was due to start the following morning.

"Went lookin' for 'im, Boss," the older jackeroo,
*Jimmy, the spokesman, told him. "Paddy has bin in a bit
of a mess. Woman trouble, Boss."*

Garrick took the chopper up again, making low sweeps
of the outstation. At first not overly concerned, he began to
feel real unease. Where the hell was Patrick? The jackeroos, from all accounts, had made a fairly extensive ground
search. He had no reason to disbelieve they hadn't. On
the contrary, he had formed the opinion that the jackeroos
had been doing the bulk of the outstation work. Either
one of them would have made a more effective manager
than O'Donnell right now. His father had wanted to give
O'Donnell a chance, but he hadn't reckoned on *woman
trouble*. It did strange things to a man.

Finally, he landed the chopper in a clearing not far from
a water channel, having decided on taking a quick search
through the bush. He was walking, hacking away at low
slung branches ready to whack him across the face. As
he went he prayed. O'Donnell was an excellent stockman
but he had never thought him remarkable for his mental
strength and resilience. Life in an outstation, deep in the
heart of a harsh environment, demanded a goodly amount
of stoicism and an abiding love of the bush. As far as he

was concerned, O'Donnell didn't really possess either. And there was always the blight of a broken love affair. That could play hell with the best of men.

Daniel had dozed off peacefully minutes after Zara closed the book she had been reading to him. The author had a marvellous prose style and a great story telling ability. They were up to page twenty-nine—there were no chapters as such—now she set the book aside, glancing at her wristwatch.

It was now three p.m. Helen had said over lunch that she expected Garrick back by one p.m. at the outside. They had received no radio message to say there was any kind of trouble on Biri Biri. Garrick would let them know if there was.

With her thirty plus years of experience of station life, Helen assured the increasingly anxious Zara that Garrick was well used to handling any number of stressful and often dangerous situations. The chopper could land almost anywhere on Biri Biri. Garrick might have had to go in search of Patrick. Mustering was due to start the following day. Maybe Patrick was working out the best site for the holding yard.

"Relax, dear," Helen cautioned. "All's well. I'm sure of it." Helen managed not to convey any sense of unease. But this was her son. Her Garrick. Truth be known, she had *always* worried about her menfolk.

"I can't help being a bit nervous, Helen," Zara said, her mind on the fragility and unpredictability of life. Some part of her had thought her father would go on for ever, yet he was gone.

"Of course you can't," Helen agreed, reaching across to take Zara's hand. "After what happened to your father."

Helen couldn't bring herself to mention Leila, who had deliberately set out to destroy Kathryn's marriage and, ultimately, *her*.

"I let him rule my life, Helen," Zara confessed with the deepest regret mixed with a sense of guilt. "I loved him. I miss him too. But he made life hard for me. He caused me a lot of grief." Deliberately too. Now, that was very hard to take.

"Well, I know he came between you and Garrick." Helen exhaled slowly.

"I was so terribly defenceless against him," Zara said. "My father, my enemy! I used to long for his attention when I was growing up. We had been robbed of our mother but, afterwards, Dad literally turned his face against me. At the same time, when he ordered me home all those years ago, I obeyed. That was always my response. Obedience."

Helen smiled grimly. "I don't think there were very many people who ignored your father's commands, dear. He never asked, like other people—he commanded. He disliked me thoroughly. I gave him cause. I've often thought Dalton's actions were a form of revenge against me and, as a consequence, revenge against my son. You love Garrick, don't you." It was a statement, not a question.

Zara felt overwhelmed by how much. "I think I started to fall in love with him when I was eight years old," she said. "He fascinated me, the 'wild bush boy'. I loved him—love him—with all my heart, but I can't forgive him for not reading even *one* of my letters, Helen, and I wrote him stacks. Poured my heart out. I would have read his."

"Would you, I wonder, Zara? Believing the man you love had cut you out of his life. Had pretended he loved you, then walked away. I suppose none of us can be sure.

But I do understand, as a woman, how you feel. The thing is, the past has to be put behind the both of you."

Zara was shaking her dark head. "Easier said than done, Helen. On one level nothing has changed. Our passion for one another. Yet on another level we're not even in the same street. Can I ask you something? I want your opinion; I value your opinion."

"Go ahead," Helen invited, reaching out to gently touch the side of Zara's cheek. "Whatever you say is in strict confidence. However long it takes to tell me, I'll hear you out."

Zara's smile was heartfelt and warm. "Thank you, Helen. It seems to me...if it were true...you could know."

"Well, let's hear it," Helen urged. "Something is clearly bothering you."

"I could tell you it has bothered me for years. Did Mummy have real difficulty conceiving, Helen? I wouldn't be surprised if she did, the way Dad was, so overbearing, so impatient for results. Men like Dad have to have an heir. There must have been a lot of stress placed on Mummy."

Helen closed her eyes, not believing what she was hearing. "But my dearest girl, Kathryn produced Corin within two years of the marriage. I wouldn't call that having *difficulty*, would you? I didn't have Garrick before two years of marriage. Ideally, husband and wife need to get to know one another, live together for a time before the children arrive. Why ever would you ask such a thing? Is it something to do with what your father told you?" A frown appeared between her well shaped brows.

Zara could hear her father's voice as though it were yesterday. "Dad said I might encounter the same difficulties falling pregnant as my mother—the same physical type, genetics, whatever. The Rylances don't have families as such. They have dynasties. He implied it could be a disaster if, in the event Garrick and I married, I mightn't be able to provide sons."

Helen was so angry she stuttered, while she looked Zara square in the eyes. "I—I—I've never heard so much *rubbish* in my born days! The *truth* was something your father didn't concern himself with. I'm sorry to have to say this, Zara, we are talking about your father, but I'm certain whatever he told you was for the express purpose of splitting you and Garrick up. Whilst you're at it, you might tell me what other falsehoods he had to spout?" Helen's blue eyes blazed.

Zara pressed her palms together. "Helen, it was as much *my* fault as his. I *believed* him. I believed I might not be cut out for childbearing, or easy childbearing. According to my father, Mummy couldn't bear the thought of facing another pregnancy. That's why there were only two of us. I believed him when I adored my mother. I *believed*— just as he intended—I wouldn't make Garrick a suitable wife for when the time came and he inherited Cooranga. Sally Forbes seemed so much more the sort of woman he needed. Dad called me a *'hothouse flower, just like your mother'*."

Helen shook her head in arrant disbelief. "A *hothouse flower* he couldn't wait to possess," she said strongly. If only Garrick had read those letters.

All the if onlys in the world!

"You don't need to blame yourself for anything, Zara," Helen continued, grasping Zara's hand in a gesture of reassurance. "You were only twenty-three years old and, in many ways, you'd led a very protected lifestyle. Your father knew well how to choose his victims." Helen's mouth tightened.

"And the scars haven't mended, Helen." Tears filled Zara's eyes. "Garrick should have had more trust in me."

"He should—he should!" Helen agreed. "But he no more understands what was happening now than then. You must see, Dalton was very clever. So was Leila. It suited their purpose whenever they saw my son on the odd occasion to give him a whole lot of misinformation. Though Garrick was always on your side, he did consider that you might not have made any attempt at making friends with Leila. You know how charming she could be when it suited her. We knew both you and Corin were deeply hostile to her. Took me no time at all to realize why. Perhaps unfortunately for you and Garrick, I gave vent to my feelings after your mother died. Dalton was not a man to forgive any form of criticism or, as he saw it, interference. I admit I went overboard. I was so upset. Daniel did warn me—but I cared deeply for your mother. So...are you going to tell Garrick all this?"

Something distant came into Zara's beautiful dark eyes. "No, I'm not, Helen." She shook her head. "Garrick might have suffered. But so did I. I can't believe at some point he didn't want to know what was in my letters. If he had opened them he might have been able to see the truth—but he said he burned the lot."

"I'm afraid he did, my dear," Helen sadly confirmed. "Daniel and I didn't interfere, not even when he got himself engaged to Sally. But we knew, of course, he'd been madly in love with you and we didn't believe he had fallen out. The reverse side of love they say, is hate. Not that he has ever hated you. Or could. Nor did he ever speak about what happened between you. But, without question I regret to say, he blamed you for the breakup. I guess he played out what happened between you over and over in his head. But there's always a solution to a problem, Zara," she said, quietly optimistic.

"Not this time." Zara shook her head. "Not unless Garrick can recover his trust in me. Wounds are wounds. I couldn't take Garrick mistrusting me in such a way again. There's no balance!" Her voice broke with emotion. "He should be back by now, surely? I think I'll go down to the airstrip and wait."

Such a gulf between the heart and the mind, Helen thought. "If you want to, dear," she said. "Don't panic. This is the Outback. Things happen all the time. Garrick will be back as soon as he is able."

CHAPTER FIVE

THE helicopter appeared as a speck in the peacock blue sky.

Thank God, thank God!

Zara had been trying to keep her anxieties within bounds, but the way her parents had died kept coming back to confront her—a tangible reminder of the transience of life! She wondered, if only for a heartbeat, if she should forgive Garrick for not having had enough belief in her, but the thing was done. They had lost valuable, irreplaceable years of their lives. It was *her* biological clock that was ticking. Men fathered children well into their seventies. The hurt Garrick had caused her was so bad she still wasn't over it. Neither was he. He had made that perfectly clear.

Her success in business had given her much needed confidence. The fact that a man like Sir Marcus Boyle had believed in her, given her a top spot in his team had acted as a spur. But then came Konrad Hartmann. The furore surrounding his illegal activities and her alleged relationship with him had caused her to slip right back. She had to ask herself—why had she become even lightly involved with Konrad? She had. The answer most likely was that powerful men had overshadowed her whole life. Powerful men took what they wanted and to hell with the consequences.

* * *

Zara watched as the rotors spun slowly to a stop. Moments later, Garrick was walking towards her, looking as vital as any man possibly could. "Zara?" His expression changed as he recognized the strain in her face. "What is it? What's the matter? Why are you wait—"

She cut him short. "Nothing's wrong, Garrick," she said, betraying the fact that her nerves were strung out like wires. "You could have let us know you were going to be delayed. You were supposed to be back by midday." It came out like the accusation it was.

Garrick's vivid blue eyes narrowed slightly. "You were worried?"

"Of course I was worried," she snapped. Her heart began to race, as a sudden surge of adrenalin swept through her body.

"What do I make of that, then?" he mocked, a twist to his handsome mouth.

"Make what you like—" she began angrily, but he reached for her. His arm closed around her back, slipped to her waist, enough strength in it to crush her.

"I'm sorry," he said. "There was really no time."

"You don't look sorry." She tried to ease the tension that racked up in her.

"What is it you want from me, Zara?" he asked.

"God knows!" Her eyes suddenly brimmed with over-wrought tears. "Forgive me. Forgive yourself. I wasn't the only one who made the biggest mistake of their life, Garrick. You did too."

"Stop. Stop now." He pulled her so tight every inch of her body was fused to his. "The last thing I wanted was to put extra strain on you. I see I have. You're not used to this way of life, Zara. Lots of dramas, I'm afraid. And after your father…"

"I know." She shuddered.

"Oh, Zara!" His hand closed hungrily around the back of her neck. He bent his head to kiss her. The degree of emotion that flared between them was more powerful than either could withstand.

"I have to come to you tonight," he muttered against her open mouth, his breath labouring under the burden of longing. "I can't go on like this, Zara. Having you so near…"

Out of the corner of her eye, she became aware that one of the station employees, a mechanic, was emerging from the hangar, wiping his grease-covered hands on a grey rag. "Someone is coming, Rick," she warned him, her heart going like a trip hammer.

He stepped back a little, still keeping his arm around her. "No problem," he said, turning his head to see who it was. "I want to have a word with Maurie anyway." Without haste, he dropped his arm, moving off to speak to the mechanic. Zara was made fully aware he wasn't in the least embarrassed by anything the man might have seen.

When he rejoined her, she went to get behind the wheel of the jeep, but he shook his head. "I'll drive."

"Okay, Boss!" She raised her hand in mock salute before sliding into the passenger seat. Just one kiss and a fine sweat had broken out on her face, her neck, funnelling into the cleft between her breasts. She began to cool off as the air conditioning kicked in.

"I have some bad news," he said when they were underway.

She felt her skin tighten. "O'Donnell?"

"No easy way to put it. Patrick arrived at the point where he felt life was no longer worth living."

Zara felt a great wrench of pity and sadness. "Ah, *no!*" she moaned. "You mean he's dead?"

"I found him near a waterhole, still holding the rifle."
Garrick said very quietly. "He had gone a good distance
from the bungalow. The boys had made a ground search.
Naturally, I had to wait until his body was airlifted to Base
Hospital."

"Oh, my God, how awful! That he should think, *This
is it! I have to die!* I'm so sorry, Garrick. I should never
have—"

"Forget it," he said. "I'm not going to tell Dad. I don't
think he could handle it in his state of health. He hasn't
got long. He's dying."

"I know."

"Aren't we all?" Garrick released a sombre breath. "I
meant what I said, Zara. I want you with me tonight." He
reached out to close his hand around her wrist. "No need
for you to be concerned about Ellie and Dad. It's an open
secret that they mean to bring us together."

"So what do *we* mean?" She turned her head to stare
at his handsome profile, sculpted in bronze.

"What can I say?" he answered quietly enough. "I don't
want you to go away."

She *knew* he was feeling the emotion, the tension of re-
membering. "Do you love me, Garrick?" she asked before
he could throw up any more defences.

"What do you expect—a simple yes or no?" he retorted,
blue eyes blazing over her. "If love means wanting you
more than anything else in the world, I guess the answer
is *yes*. But it's not about *me*, Zara, is it? It was never about
me. I might have the effect on you of a magnet but are
you a *stayer*? That's the thing. We mightn't have your
father around to contend with. He called, you jumped.
But I won't go through the same experience as last time.
You're either with me or you're *not*! And I'm not going
to give you all the time in the world to decide."

"And you're sorry for nothing?" she shot back, thoroughly on edge.

"Sure I'm sorry," he said.

She forced herself to pause and take stock. A man—a *young* man—had died, for God's sake! A young man who had woken up that morning and made a wrong final decision. "You've had a bad day, Garrick," she said, humble apology in her voice. "This isn't the time to speak about our problems. They never seem to go away. You're going to tell your mother about Patrick?"

He nodded wearily. "Of course. Ellie is the very last person to want to upset Dad. I'll just say O'Donnell quit. That's what he did, didn't he?" He threw her a glance full of the awareness of inescapable human suffering. "He simply *quit*. I suppose his girlfriend won't even remember him in a year's time. Maybe less."

Zara looked down at her linked hands, needing to say something for this woman who couldn't yet speak for herself. "You don't know that, Garrick," she said. "There are always reasons why things don't work."

"I suppose," he groaned. "I've become very cynical, God help me!" He turned his head to pin her dark lustrous gaze. "Come down to me tonight. Or I'll come and get you."

Excitement was in the acceleration of her heartbeat. "You're not going to allow me to make the decision?"

"No," he said. He couldn't have sounded more emphatic.

There was something about the expression in Daniel Rylance's eyes that spoke of many long years of experience and understanding of the human condition. They had finished dinner; now they were sitting in the Garden Room, where the housekeeper had served coffee.

"O'Donnell didn't quit, did he?" Daniel focused on his son, who had actually been waiting for one of his father's direct questions.

Garrick lowered his coffee cup very slowly. "Never could fool you, Dad."

"The truth, son. The truth about what happened."

"I won't have you upset yourself, Daniel," Helen strongly intervened.

"Hush, woman. I can handle it," Daniel told his wife gently.

Zara had had exactly the same thought as Helen, but Garrick acceded to his father's request.

"I thought he'd be up for it; up for the challenge," Daniel said when Garrick had finished an account that left out the worst moments.

"He would have been, Dad, only none of us realised how far this thing had gone between him and his girlfriend."

"The poor girl has to be notified," Helen said. Zara had since been told that Patrick had never known his white father. His mother, part Aboriginal, had long since disappeared from his life. Coorango had been his home since the age of sixteen. "Patrick may have contributed to the cause of the break up. He did have his problems. We can't blame the girl."

"Well, we might never know," said Daniel. "I don't say this against poor Patrick…" He stopped mid-flight, his expression full of sorrow. Then he continued. "Daniel came to us a homeless boy. He was happy here for years, an excellent worker. Then he finds a girlfriend who maybe, just maybe, makes him feel like nothing. God, I don't know. But it seems to me young people these days don't seem to have the fight in them that we did. One can't get through life without obstacles getting in the way. For some people it's on a daily basis. One obstacle after the other to hurdle. No use to duck them. Better face them head on. You've told the men?" He looked to Garrick.

Garrick nodded. "Believe it or not, the Aboriginal stockmen already had wind of it," Garrick said. "Now, you must leave everything to me, Dad."

Daniel frowned, shook his head imperceptibly, then he nodded. "Will do, son."

Zara could see herself standing like a hapless virgin in the hallway outside Garrick's suite of rooms. She really did need help. She was making no move to go closer, to knock on his door. In fact, she was beginning to feel light-headed. Should she go back the way she had come? No point in that. Garrick had said he would come looking for her. He *would*. God knew, she wanted to be found. Warily, one step at a time, she drew closer. What was wrong with her? If it weren't so pathetic it would have been laughable. She and Garrick had made love countless times. But that was years ago. Their coming together after the wedding and into the early hours of the next day had been a passionate, borderline *furious* attempt to wrest something from the other.

Poor old you! The promised happy ever after never came about.

She was wearing an exquisite ivory satin nightgown and a matching satin robe, very luxurious and sensual. She might as well have been naked, so conscious was she of her flesh stirring. Garrick's parents occupied a suite in the west wing. Garrick's suite of rooms was entirely private in the east wing of the huge homestead. There were five double bedrooms to each wing. In the old days before Daniel's horrendous accident there were always guests at Coorango. There would be guests for the Trophy week-end when Garrick's ex-fiancée who was having marital problems would be in residence. Helen seemed to think Sally might make an advance or two. Would she? There was no accounting for what men and women got up to. Illicit relationships were legendary.

Daniel and Helen had long since retired. The homestead was in darkness. Yet she crept along the wide gallery, a spectacular part of the house, as though the bedrooms were occupied and guests would open their doors to question where she was going.

If one wanted the truth, she had to work exceptionally hard at being a femme fatale. She couldn't believe the London press had labelled her that. *A femme fatale!* They couldn't have been more off track. Any chance she might have had at being a femme fatale had been destroyed early on. It wouldn't be an exaggeration to say her father had done his best to put a blowtorch to her self-confidence. Physical abuse was horrible. Emotional abuse had serious consequences as well.

God, I'm so nervous!

Miranda had once told her that when she was nervous she tried whistling. Even thinking of Miranda made her smile. She couldn't whistle in any case. Whistling wasn't one of her skills.

No need to knock hard on the door. Tap. It wasn't as though she was arriving unannounced. Only it was a very heavy mahogany door. Would he hear? She was a seething mass of insecurities. Too much vulnerability, especially for a woman her age. She knew the outside world saw her as one thing—a young woman with everything she could possibly want. Had they ever seen *inside* her highly dysfunctional family, it might have been quite an eye-opener. No one needed a father who lived to intimidate.

Just as she was staring at the gleaming door knob, one hand poised to grasp it, the door suddenly opened wide.

Garrick stood with his back against the light—very tall, blazing blue eyes offset by his dark colouring and bronze tan, his physique little short of magnificent. He was still wearing what he had on at dinner—a collarless ice-white linen shirt, albeit most of the buttons now undone, long sleeves rolled to the elbow, narrow dress jeans and hand-tooled boots. He might have been a movie star cowboy, purring masculine sexuality. "You weren't thinking of staying out there, I trust?" he asked, putting a hand to her arm.

"Actually, I was in two minds."

"Were you indeed?" He drew her into his bedroom, which could have been split into two huge rooms. It was very much *gentleman's quarters*, all gleaming dark cabinetry and furnishings, the timber offset by lots of white. A spirited desert wind was blowing through the open French windows, making the sheer white inner curtains dance. Scorchingly hot by day, the desert cooled off fast at night. The breeze was delicious, the scent of the native boronia rising like incense.

Garrick closed the door, then set her against it, arms to either side of her, locking her in. "That is the most beautiful nightdress I've ever seen." His eyes slid down over her body. It was quivering so much he might have made physical contact. "It's almost a pity I have to take it off you."

"Why on earth would you want to do that?" she countered.

He smiled. "Just kidding. You can keep it on. For the moment. Why, oh why, are you so nervous, Zara?" He stared deep into her lustrous dark eyes. "You never used to be."

"That was a lifetime ago," she reminded him.

"Indeed. Then and now are different lifetimes. You

were one shameless hussy in those days, flaunting your nakedness when we were skinny-dipping in the lagoon. Ah, those passionate interludes!" He began to drag kisses down the column of her neck, the tip of his tongue against her scented skin. "What a difference the years bring."

She made no response, feeling the enormous pull of his gravity. Her breath was tightening, shortening as, unhurriedly, he let his hands slide over her body, every movement inventive, flicking a little electric switch. She couldn't control the soft little moans of pleasure that escaped her. This man was her downfall. She turned to putty in his hands.

"I'm still as mad about you as I ever was. Madder." There was an edge of self-mockery in his tone. "I guess a psychiatrist would call it a fixation. You know, the one blind spot in an otherwise clear and controlled mind." He raised his darkly glossy head. "It's not a name I care to mention—I promise I'll only say it *one* more time. *Did* you sleep with Hartmann?"

Zara didn't reply. Trust was sacred. He didn't have it.

"So I can take that as a yes?"

Her eyes were suddenly full of fire. "Let me ask you a similar question, though I'm certain I know the answer. Have you any memory of sleeping with Sally?"

He didn't miss a beat. "She *was* my fiancée."

"So I take that as a yes?"

The expression on his face was wry. "Sally was—is—a very sweet girl. Most likely I didn't deserve anyone so sweet and understanding. With all your faults, you were more my speed. I thought I could love Sally. I couldn't. Though I spent a fair bit of time trying to convince myself. Didn't work. Wasn't fair to Sally. The problem was, not a woman in the world has your incomparable ability to bring me to my knees."

She regarded him in silence for a moment. "And you couldn't deal with it."

"What?" he mocked. "I couldn't de—"

She cut him off. "An abiding characteristic of yours is *pride*. Pride is one of the deadly sins."

He laughed suddenly, unexpectedly, the most attractive, seductive sound. "I dare say it is. Have you come to pick a fight, Zara, my darling?"

"I want to understand you," she said with intensity. "You ask about Konrad Hartmann. *I'll* say this only one more time. He was not my lover. Nor would I have accepted him as a lover. He took me out a few times. Kissed me. Let's leave it at that."

"I find it very hard to believe *he* could." The violent rush of jealousy Garrick felt startled him.

"You don't trust what I say?" She stared into his blazing eyes. Backlit sapphires couldn't have looked more blue or brilliant.

"You're a very beautiful woman, Zara. He had to have *tried*?"

She shook her head. Her long sable hair, flowing down her back, rippled with the movement. "Konrad was never impertinent. He wasn't a man who would ever need to deploy force." She knew as she spoke she was winding Garrick up. It didn't overly concern her. It was more payback time.

"You have no trouble talking about him?" Garrick asked suavely.

"*You're* the one having the trouble, Rick."

"I guess I am." His mouth curved down.

"Trust is enormously important. Perhaps *the* most important thing. You don't have trust in me. Maybe you never will."

Garrick raised a hand, his expression one of ironic reproof. "So is this what it's all about? You'll never forgive me for not opening your letters?"

"It was a major mistake."

He dropped the humour. "Okay, I admit it. You have every right to be shocked and upset. But sometimes it's extremely difficult to regain what is lost. I loved you so much. I gave full rein to my passion. I would have trusted you with my life. Maybe what I did was unforgivable, but pain has a way of lodging itself inside your brain. Pain became a part of me. I'm not a man who takes kindly to being betrayed. *You* were the one who set things in motion, Zara. Assigning blame seems pretty damned complicated to me. What *did* you say in your letters, anyway?"

She took exception to his tone. "Reasons for my behaviour," she said pointedly.

He made a gesture of infinite impatience. "So we're going to talk on our feet, are we? At least we can lie down and slog it out." He swooped, lifting her off her feet as though she were weightless, and carried her to his bed. Custom built to the scale of a big man, Zara thought as she tumbled across the sheets—not even crumpled—fresh, clean, smelling again of the wild boronia with its prized perfume.

Garrick bounced down so heavily beside her that her light body with its coltishly long slender limbs almost became airborne. He put his hands behind his handsome head, his crow-black hair glossy and springy with health, staring at the plaster ceiling with its beautiful mouldings and central rose. A handsome bronze and rock crystal chandelier was appended from the rose, casting its light across the entire room.

"Can we have that off?" she asked, putting up a hand as though the brilliance was blinding her. God help her, she was shy as well.

"No," he replied shortly, a brooding expression on his handsome countenance. "I want to look at you. Every inch of you. I want to be absolutely sure it *is* you beside me in bed. Multiple personalities and all! Now, where were we?"

She heaved herself up, leaning over him. Her hair fanned out all around her face, cascading over her shoulders and curling into sinuous loops onto his chest. "Would you want me if I couldn't give you children?"

His whole demeanour changed dramatically. Before she knew what he was about, he had her on her back, staring down at her, a vertical line between his black brows. "What are you talking about?" His gaze was super-alert and penetrating. "Do you think you may have a problem? Do you *know*?"

"No, actually, I don't." She sighed. "I'm just asking."

"God, Zara, I don't know what I'm going to do about you," he said. "Let's turn this on its head. What if *I* had a problem? Would you marry me?"

"Garrick, you're the embodiment of masculinity." Her beautiful dark eyes were filled with sudden melancholy. "My father tried to convince me I could have difficulty conceiving."

"Hang on, hang on." Garrick was roused to anger. "He did *what*?"

He sounded incredulous, maybe doubting. She turned her head away. "He said my mother had difficulty conceiving Corin and me. She found having children so threatening she didn't want any more after us."

"And your *father* told you this?" He greeted that with outright aggression.

"He made it sound as if it were out of regard for you. I told you in a letter, if only you'd read it."

Garrick's expression was truly daunting. "I could murder him."

"Too late."

"But Zara, you're exceptionally intelligent." His voice became gentle. He moved a silky wisp of hair skeined across her cheek. "Why did you believe it? Why didn't you get yourself checked out? Obviously, the thought has weighed heavily on you. Was it even true, anyway, about your mother? I don't, for one, accept it. She was wonderful with children. I saw her. She loved children. They loved her. I suppose she could have had a bad time in childbirth. I wouldn't know. Why don't you ask Ellie? There's not much my mother doesn't know.'

"I *have* asked her. She won't have a word of it. But then Helen makes no bones about what she thought of my father."

"And this was your fear? Seriously. For real?"

"For real," she told him flatly. "Or one of them. My father played me. He didn't care. He thought nothing of the difficulties I might have in the future. Most definitely he didn't want *you* for a son-in-law."

"Of course not!" Garrick gave a bark of laughter. "He wanted a son-in-law he could push around. But if you loved me, Zara, you would have married me regardless. So what other bombshells do you have in your arsenal?" He fell back against the pilled up pillows, sighing deeply.

"You never did ask me to marry you."

He sat up again, the glint of anger in his fabulous face. "I think I spoke about when we were married ten thousand times. If you'd have hung around I would have gone down on bended knee. As it happened, the minute my back was turned, you took off. Isn't that so, my beautiful Zara?" he taunted her. "Zara, the runaway. A most dishonourable departure."

"It was in its way," she admitted. She had caught the freight plane when Garrick was in Darwin for a couple of days on business for his father. Made up some excuse about her father needing her to sign papers, whatever.

"You want to explain that a bit more?"

"No," she said. "Of the two of us, I had the roughest deal."

"Sez you! Anyway, why don't we check it out?" He sounded very matter-of-fact.

"Check what out?" She gripped his arm, her eyes huge.

"How quickly you can fall pregnant." He gazed back at her with open challenge.

"I am *not* going to fall pregnant. Just for the moment. I don't really think I like you." She pretended interest in the rock crystals in the chandelier.

His mouth curved into an enigmatic smile. "Liking isn't necessary for you-know-what. All right then, a postpone-ment. But you will consider it?"

"Are you serious or joking?" she asked cautiously.

"I couldn't be more serious." As though arriving at a decision, he threw his long legs off the bed, stood straight. Then he began stripping off his clothes, making short work of it. "I *will* make you pregnant, Zara. Have no fear of that. It's your inevitable fate. But it's all a question of commit-ment, isn't it? I'm assuming you want my child?'

"We could have had two or three by now," she flashed back. Her dark gaze fixed on his splendid male body was anguished. God, he was a glorious man! The classic model for splendid male sculpture. Height, strength, ridges of rippling muscle. Dominant sexuality. She was desperate and exhilarated at one and the same time. She wanted him to seize her, make passionate love to her, make a baby.

And there was something else. She attempted to identify it. Something quite profound. Ah, yes! She no longer believed a word her father had said, even if it had taken a ferociously long time.

"Move over." Garrick gave the order, the flush of blood in his striking face. "I'm going to undress you. V-e-r-y slowly." He turned her head towards him. Then he bent to touch, taste, then fully capture her mouth in a long ravishing kiss that gave her a huge buzz.

"Behold, you are beautiful, my love," he murmured, lifting his mouth momentarily from hers. "My love, my dove, my one desire. Your breasts are perfect white roses, tipped with pink. You're impossibly beautiful." His voice was very gentle, yet fantastically seductive.

Sensation was growing, *e-x-p-a-n-d-i-n-g* inside her. Her long slender legs began moving restlessly of their own accord. Ripples of excitement passed over her. Heat flared at the delta of her body. He placed his hand very gently over the pulsing area, fingers dipping into the tender cleft. "Zara?" Brilliant blue eyes questioned.

"I never could resist you." Her head felt so heavy she thought she couldn't lift it off the pillow. Her whole body was heavy. Heavy and deeply languorous with desire.

"So let's make your robe disappear." He turned her on her side. "We might dawdle over the nightgown. I feel like kissing you through the satin."

She was lying on her back again, staring up at him, her flesh responding to his teasing, highly provocative ministrations. He touched his mouth to each breast in turn, the nipples exquisitely sensitised, bunched tight like berries. "Five years. *Five years*, Zara!" he groaned. "Is it any wonder there's so much hurt in me?"

Her eyes, which had been shut against such thrilling sensation, opened. Her voice rose up from within her, vibrating with desire. "Make love to me, Rick," she gasped. "I'm serious here. Before I go up in smoke!"

"My, my, my!" he drawled, turning her so he could align her body with his. Man. Woman. His arms enfolding her. "So impatient! I'm going to spin this out for a little while. Go to sleep if you want," he mocked.

"You're a devil...a devil..." Spasms of excitement were shooting through her, stifled little moans.

He began to draw her satin nightdress over her head; she shifted her weight to make it easy for him. "No devil, Zara," he said. "Just a fool for love."

CHAPTER SIX

LIGHT aircraft arriving mid-morning announced the big sporting event on the Outback calendar, the Sinclair Cup. It was the perfect day for the match—a cobalt blue sky with a single puffball cloud on the horizon and a welcome cooling breeze blowing right across the plains country and the rolling grasslands. Numerous creeks and streams were in flow after better than expected spring rains added moisture to the atmosphere. There was even a good deal more shade around the polo field. The bauhinias were in abundance pink, white and cerise, scattering a ring of spent blossom like multicoloured confetti. Many of the gums were sporting masses of sweet blossom in pendant branches of hot orange and smouldering scarlet. Even the shimmering heat mirage was floating mid-air.

Many more people, competitors, guests and spectators, had made the trek overland in safaris of dusty four-wheel drives, covered trucks and buses. There were refreshments awaiting them in several of the huge marquees with their bright bunting and streamers that had been positioned around the grounds. Excitement was in the air. Lots of smiling faces, the mingling of many voices. It promised to be a thrilling match with both teams sporting superb players. Garrick was captain of the Blue Team. Moss Northrop was long time captain of the Red Team. It was going to be quite a battle. Both men were very, very tough competitors. The lead up match, with players of less outstanding handicaps but plenty of drive, would start after the lavish barbecue lunch on offer starting at noon. The main match was scheduled for three p.m.

By noon the whole area was crammed, the excited crowd taking great delight in an occasion that brought Outback people together from across a huge area of the South-West. The Polo Ball would start at eight p.m. a dance to dawn affair. Breakfast would be provided from first light. It was just the *best* time! Greatly appreciated by all. Such times brought everyone together in friendship.

Or so one would have hoped.

But there was always the exception to keep events balanced.

Helen had put Sally and Nick Draper into one of the guest rooms in the West Wing. It was a beautiful big room, sunshine-yellow and white with touches of sapphire blue with an adjoining en suite bathroom, but one would have thought it was a broom closet, so sour was the expression on Sally Draper's attractively angular, lightly tanned face. Zara, obeying Helen's instructions, had escorted Sally to it, seeing there was a new version of Sally Draper. Sally had developed a very hard edge, though it had not been apparent in Helen's company. Rather the reverse. Sally had been all sweetness and light.

Safely inside the guest bedroom, it was a different story. Sally started right in without a breather. "It was a *huge* surprise to hear you were staying here," she said, her hazel eyes as clear and cold as Antarctic waters.

Zara felt the tide of dislike like an approaching tsunami. From what little she had seen of Sally, she had formed the opinion that she was a very pleasant young woman. Obviously Sally had undergone a remarkable sea change.

"Why is that?" Zara kept her tone mild with an act of will. Anyone would have thought she was personally responsible for Sally's marriage problems.

Sally's tanned cheeks turned bright pink. "Why so coy? I really don't need that. We're of an age. You know perfectly well you're the one who broke Garrick's heart. Made quite a job of it too. He couldn't settle for me. Oh, no! Not after you, with the magnolia skin and the big, big black eyes." She looked Zara full in the face. "So what are you doing back here?"

"Well, hello to you too, Sally," Zara managed, wryly. This had nothing to do with Sally's husband at all. "I'm a guest here—what else? Surely *you* don't give a damn either way?" Slow to anger, Zara could feel her temper rising. "I appreciate you were once engaged to Garrick, Sally, but you're now a happily married woman."

"Whoa there!" Sally, splendid horsewoman that she was, held up a restraining hand. "Last time I looked, my marriage was a goddamned mess."

"And you're looking for someone to blame?" Zara's question was almost gentle. She wanted no part of a confrontation.

"Don't be smart!" Sally warned. "I had a dream and it went up in smoke." It couldn't have been plainer that Sally was hurting.

"Then I'm sorry to hear it," Zara said, slowly and carefully. "Can't you work your way through a bad patch?"

Sally gave a near equine snort of disgust. "You're a great one for offering advice. Tell me, are you planning on dumping Garrick again?"

Zara found herself more angry on Garrick's behalf than her own. She wanted to hit back. But reined herself in. "That's really none of your business, Sally. I never *dumped* Rick, as you call it. Rick isn't exactly the sort of man one dumps."

"Not the way *I* heard it," Sally retorted, a granite edge to her voice. "Garrick told me all about you. I had to listen for hours. But I did. I guess it was a sort of therapy for him."

"Nonsense!" Zara reacted smartly. "No matter what Rick thought of me I know him too well to believe what you say."

"Oh, God, don't kid yourself," Sally sneered, immense jealousy in her eyes. "He told me you were totally devoid of regret or remorse. You promised to marry him—strung him along—then you bolted like a thief in the night."

Zara stared back at Sally for a few moments. "I did. I made the worst possible mistake. But you don't know the real truth of the matter."

"I know you were too gutless to tell him you were just playing around," Sally said, a touch of hysteria in her eyes. "The over-privileged, over-pampered Daddy's little girl."

Zara released a pent-up sigh, wondering if there was any backup within call. Not that she wanted Helen or the housekeeper, Madge Jensen, to hear quarrelling voices. The day had started so well. "You're nowhere near the truth, Sally. Not even a close approximation. I was *never* a Daddy's girl. I do wish you'd stop trying to stir things up. It's so sad."

Sally stood defiant, a bitter jealousy lodged like a tumour near her heart. "There are plenty of things I could tell you that you wouldn't want to hear."

"Watch your own back, Sally," Zara advised. "You really shouldn't be bringing your problems to the Trophy

Weekend. This is one of the big highlights of the year. It might help you to remember that."

Sally bunched her fists together; the knuckles showed white. She looked strong, very fit, tall like Zara, but with a lethal twist. "Stop trying to play the countrywoman," she said with a tight malicious smile. "You could never manage out here. Not in a million light years." She moved a foot or two back, suddenly plonking down on the king-size bed. "I still love him, you know," she said and grabbed a silk cushion as though she wanted to pitch it at Zara's head. "I'll always love him."

Sadly, Zara believed her. "Yet you married Nick?" What a rough deal Nick got, then!

Sally gave a bitter laugh. "Nick is an admirable guy, but he's no Garrick. Garrick takes out the honours for *everything*. Makes a man impossible to forget. But *you*!" She looked up at Zara with near hatred. "I knew in my bones you were going to turn up. Sooner or later. You're the sort of femme fatale who marks her territory."

Here we go again. The femme fatale label.

Zara said a silent prayer. *Dear Lord, keep me calm.* "Sally, you're going too far now," she said, firming up her voice. "Seriously, I don't want to listen. In fact, the very last thing I want is to have this painful discussion with you. The femme fatale label is a piece of nonsense. I'm just like any other woman."

"Yeah?" Sally continued to glare back. "Well, we all know what happened to you in England. Got yourself mixed up with a world class crook. The word *mistress* springs to mind."

Zara gave a heartfelt sigh. "Anyone that knows me didn't buy that. I had no special relationship with Konrad Hartmann—I just got caught up in the media frenzy. The media don't have strict rules like sticking to the truth.

Anyway, let me point out again, it's none of your business. I've half a mind to get Rick up here to straighten things out." It was an empty threat. She had no such intention. But Sally was really getting to her. She felt herself undeserving of the insults Sally was throwing around.

"No problem!" Sally retorted with extraordinary intensity. She didn't appear at all fazed. It was more a *bring it on!* "You're as shallow as they come, Zara Rylance. Oh, you might be beautiful and clever in the Rylance way, but you're the sort of woman who goes through life causing a lot of damage. Garrick fell hard for you but he deserved a whole lot better."

"Like *you?*" Zara asked somberly, not raising her voice.

Sally had been spitting words out so vehemently she was short of breath. "We could have worked things out," she muttered, frustration and unhappiness boiling in her.

Zara shook her head. This was one unhappy, bitter young woman. "Far better, Sally, to make your marriage work, don't you think? You have moved on. Garrick has moved on. You have no chance of winning him back. I say this to spare you any humiliation. I know what it's like to suffer."

"Ah, come on, I don't believe that," Sally jeered. "You've got *everything*! But you won't get Garrick. There's no shortage of girls out there dying for Garrick to look at them. Plenty of them are here today, looking their very best. A lot of them will be at the Ball. You walked away from Garrick. Correction, you *flew* away from him. He'll never trust you again. He told me. You have quite a history, Zara Rylance."

"None of which is *your* problem." Zara turned to walk to the door. "I'm here on Coorango because Daniel and

Helen want me here. I'm here because *Garrick* wants me here."

Sally all but leapt off the bed. "A sexual relationship doesn't mean much if he doesn't ask you to marry him," she challenged, a furious light in her eyes. "Put it any way you like—you don't belong out here. An opinion based on fact. You have no real idea what Outback life is like. I took that very point up with Garrick when we were engaged. He agreed. You're the original hothouse flower. We don't grow hothouse roses in the desert. So here's a piece of advice for you, now you're so kindly handing advice around. You have your bit of fun but go away. Just like you did the last time."

Walking back down the corridor, Zara couldn't help thinking that Sally's visit brought bad karma.

She had plenty of time to count the good-looking husband-hunting young women who sat on folding camp chairs beneath the shade of the trees or under the specially installed green and white striped awnings, watching the match of the day. Polo was an elite sport, difficult and dangerous, with rules much like hockey. Each team tried to score goals by hitting the ball through the opponents goalposts using long mallets. The game had a huge following in the Outback. That afternoon the crowd abandoned themselves to highly enthusiastic bravos that resounded around the grounds, inciting each team to do their darnedest to gain supremacy.

Garrick, as captain of the Blue Team playing on his home ground, was causing much of the excitement. Apart from being compulsively watchable, he looked outrageously sexy in his polo gear—dark blue helmet, blue and white jersey piped with black, snowy-white breeches, high glossy black boots. His contribution was suffused with a kind of animal excitement. The crowd adored him, especially the female spectators with their minds simultaneously on the Gala Ball, when they would be wearing their most glamorous evening dresses. They rarely found a better opportunity to show off.

Moss Northrop, a superior player with a wide range of strokes who played far more regularly than Garrick, stood six foot five in his socks. Not surprising then that he had tremendous power play. Moss came in for his fair share of encouraging calls and strenuous clapping. Many in the crowd were wearing either blue or red rosettes to show their allegiance to their particular team, so a good deal of good-natured joshing was going on. Moss was doing his level best to disrupt the opposing captain's play or, at the very least, slow him up. He had quite a job on his hands. Garrick's play that afternoon was quite simply heroic—wrists like steel, his speed in thought and action unmatched.

The goal that won the match—a wonderful full free swing—brought every last spectator to their feet, ablaze with admiration. It had been a thrilling finish. The Blue Team had won by a margin of just one.

Well played! Well played!

Onya, Rick!

Onya, Mossie!

Helen, amid more vociferous cheering, presented the cup to her beloved son with a very proud Daniel watching from his wheelchair.

"Intelligence did it," Daniel told Zara in a proud aside. Zara had been watching the match alongside Helen and Daniel and a group of their closest friends. "Intelligence and speed," Daniel said. "Finesse beats rough house every time. Garrick would have made a professional player under different circumstances. I don't think I've seen him play a faster game."

"I'm sure *I* haven't," Zara said. "Here or anywhere else, for that matter. But I have to admit I had my heart in my throat at times." She managed a little laugh, but she had felt a weight come off her when the game finished. An interested and informed spectator of many games of polo at home and in England, it hadn't been a whole lot of fun for her watching Garrick in such dangerous action. She didn't think she would ever learn to take in her stride his pounding down field, his brilliant polo pony in the last chukka, a bay gelding, its burnished hide buffed to perfection, only two legs on the ground, with Garrick half out of the saddle, swinging his mallet. There was too much pressure when the player was a loved one. Or for her anyway.

Daniel, on the other hand, a wonderful player himself in his day, looked so much better for all the excitement. There was colour in his sunken cheeks. "Well, I don't know about you, Zara, my dear, but I'm ready to celebrate," he announced. Always fond of Zara, they had grown ever closer.

"And so we should." Zara bent to kiss his cheek. "It's been a great day." Turning the wheelchair preparatory to pushing off to the nearest marquee, Daniel stopped her, a finger up, beckoning her down to him. "I would have thought Sally would go up to Nick first," he said very quietly.

"That's a bit worrying," Zara agreed.

"Indeed it is. There she is, beaming at Garrick. Hello!" He released a whistling breath. "She's *kissing* him."

Zara nodded solemnly, far from blind. "So she is." And not on the cheek either. Fair and square on the mouth, tightening her arms around his neck. Sally appeared animated, vibrant, brimming with life. Almost ecstatic. She might as well have shouted aloud, *I still love him... love him...love him!*

"Goodness me, that must be hard on poor old Nick," Daniel said with considerable sympathy for the man. "No way to save a foundering marriage. That was no ordinary congratulatory kiss. I think I'll have a word with Garrick. Advise extreme caution. Poor Sally is still carrying a torch for him"

"More like waving a flag," Zara made the wry comment. Nick Draper, who had played extremely hard for the Red Team, was standing towelling his damp head. For the moment he was quite alone. No proud wife had rushed to his side. "Nick does look a bit miserable," Zara said and meant it.

"And I don't think it's because his team lost."

There was a reply to that. Zara didn't make it. Didn't need to. Any number of people in the large crowd who hadn't as yet headed off to the marquees had observed that kiss in jaw-dropping amazement. Sally might have been engaged to Garrick at one time but that was history. She had taken the next step and married Nick Draper.

"What Nick ought to do is march his wife off," said Daniel with a frown.

"I was going to say the same thing." She thought Garrick had drawn back. Infinitesimally, maybe. Had he? She had to remember Sally had once lain in Garrick's arms. They had been lovers. Could all that feeling simply drain away?

"Great minds think alike, my dear." Daniel sighed, then rallied. "Well, come on now. We both deserve a glass of champagne. Ellie and Garrick will join us presently."

"Ten dollars Sally tries to join in?"

Daniel laughed. "That's a considerable sum, my girl.

All right, you're on. It's up to Nick to take the next step. No man delights in public humiliation."

The Ball was in full swing by ten o'clock.

"God, you look wonderful. Totally wonderful!" Nash Beresford, a member of Garrick's team, exclaimed dramatically the instant he saw her. "It's great to see your beautiful face around here. There's not a woman here tonight to touch you." Nash had felt compelled to race to her side the instant she was free. Time now for all those other guys to lay off.

"Still talking hyperbole, Nash?" Zara smiled, not taking him seriously. There were many very pretty young women in lovely evening dresses to light up the Great Hall where traditionally the station's big functions were held.

"The truly astounding thing is you're not in the least vain. How is that?" Nash asked, all fired up just to be back with her. He had never forgotten Zara Rylance.

"I'm not altogether sure I have anything to be vain about, Nash." Zara smiled.

"And the dress!" He stood back to admire it. "It works wonderfully if you have the figure for it, which obviously you have, you lucky girl! Haute couture, of course?"

"Vintage Christian Dior," Zara said proudly. "I came by it in Paris. Paid quite a price, but I had to have it."

"And it was worth every penny," Nash said, his eyes moving very slowly over her.

Zara's gown was indeed beautiful and very feminine in the Dior style. The chiffon material was a lovely shade hard to describe. Perhaps a misty lilac—palest pink? It was cut like a slip with wide shoulder bands. It clung all the way to the hips where it flared into a floaty handkerchief hem. The bodice plunged to a subtle low, requiring small perfect breasts, the chiffon appliquéd with beaded and sequinned lace in a delicate seashell motif. Another wide band began at the hips and extended to within a foot of the hem. She wore her hair loose, the way Garrick liked it, but much fuller and more dramatic for the evening, as was her flawless make-up. Stunning pink diamonds from Western Australia's famous Argyle diamond mines swung from her ears, a twenty-first birthday present from her maternal grandparents. Normally not a fusser, she had fussed and fussed over her appearance, needing Garrick to find her beautiful. She hadn't felt any flash of jealousy when Sally had launched her breathless kiss, yet somehow she felt put on her mettle.

"You're going to dance with me?" Nash asked, watching her with open fascination.

"I'd love to." It was true. Up to a point. Across the broad expanse of the lavishly decorated Great Hall there was a non-stop, palpable explosion of female interest around Garrick. Not a woman at the Ball who didn't feel the sheer electric impact of the man. It was a black tie affair but the colour of the dinner jacket was optional, black or white. Garrick wore summer white against which his dark colouring and brilliant blue eyes were startling. So far he hadn't danced with Sally, who wore a strapless sequinned sage-green designer creation that arguably wasn't quite her colour. Zara thought a deeper shade of green but the dress was striking. Without appearing to, she had been keeping a close eye on proceedings. Sally and Nick had, in fact, arrived fairly late, Sally as though she was handcuffed to her husband. Zara feared they might have had a serious argument.

"So exactly what circumstances bring you back to Coorango?" Nash asked, gutting his arm around Zara's narrow waist and leading her out onto the dance floor. He felt absolutely chuffed. Zara Rylance always had been a knockout. If possible, she was even more beautiful. And an heiress to boot. If those two things didn't work for a girl, what would?

"Well, we are kin," she pointed out lightly. "Helen and Daniel invited me."

"What about Garrick?" Nash asked with keen interest.

"What about Garrick?" she returned sweetly.

He fastened his light blue eyes on hers. "I always had the idea you and Garrick sort of…"

"Sort of?" She didn't help him out.

"Well, you know. That was before he got engaged to Sally, of course. But what could Sally possibly offer after *you*?"

She gave him a surprised look of censure. "How ungallant! I thought you were friends with the Drapers?"

"So I am." Nash, a good-looking well-built young man, coloured slightly. My point is, Zara, you and Garrick were perfectly matched. Know what I mean? There are lots of good things to be said about Sally. Can't think of a lot offhand. Nick's no fool, you know."

"Why don't you get it off your chest?" Zara said with a challenge hard to miss.

"You must have seen them come in," Nash defended his position. "I'd have said a serious marital contretemps. I'm surprised there wasn't a black eye in sight. Not many people missed Sally's fiercely joyous and, I have to say, proprietorial kiss. Those that missed it *heard* about it."

"Excitement, nothing else." Zara was determined to downplay the incident. "Sally is a renowned horsewoman. She loves the game."

"Watch her," Nash advised. "That's my advice."

Zara felt a slight tremor. "Oh, you think she's planning something?"

"Just having a bit of fun!" Nash backed off somewhat. "Don't go riding with her. She could look for a way to make you come a cropper."

That would be easy enough for Sally to do if ever she were fool enough to join Sally in a gallop. As it was, Zara responded lightly, "However did you get to be so suspicious, Nash?"

He looked at her with genuine concern. "Zara, sweetie, I saw the way she kissed him. Poor old Nick could well be the casualty of this marriage. He's a really nice guy. Maybe too nice."

"No point in our dwelling on it, Nash. It isn't really our business. At best, it was excitement on Sally's part. At worst, she forgot herself."

"Exactly!" said Nash. "There are some really big changes going on in society. A lot aren't bothering to get married at all these days. Everyone has a *partner*. Others can't hack more than about eighteen months after tying the knot. Can't say I'm surprised here. Sally got married on the rebound."

As Garrick approached Nash handed Zara over with a single request. "Promise me another dance?"

"I think I can manage that." Zara smiled back at him.

"You're always surrounded," Nash reminded her.

"I *promise*," she said, going smoothly into Garrick's arms. He was much taller than Nash. Held her very differently. More securely. In the old days, when they had attended quite a few Outback balls, Garrick had been a marvellous dancer. A natural with innate rhythm, his tall body imbued with male grace.

The music from a top group especially flown in for the occasion was eddying all around them, spilling from a grand piano, a double bass, drums, a great clarinet and sax and, for a lot of the numbers, a fabulous guitar. "Flirting your head off with Nash?" Garrick drew her in close with a sigh of pleasure that bordered on deep relief. "He's always had a crush on you."

Shadows flitted across her face. "Well, what about you?"

"Crush?" he scoffed, drawing back a little to gaze into her lustrous dark eyes. "More a full-blown passion, wouldn't you say?" The shadow on her lids, he saw, matched the colour of her delicately seductive dress. Her mouth was so beautiful and soft, a deep but harmonising pink. Did she know what a picture she made?

"I'm not talking about *me!*" There was a definite sparkle in her eyes.

He lowered his head, his cheek pressed against hers. Then he gave a little groan into her ear. "If you start talking about Sally giving way to a mad urge to kiss me I think I'll lose it."

"You appear totally in control." She resisted the urge to throw both arms around his neck *à la* Sally. "I did see you try to pull away, though. Well, maybe a bare inch."

"Zara, my love, please don't let's talk about Sally," he begged. "I feel truly sorry for her. This is supposed to be a festive occasion."

"And so it is," she returned, light and fire still in her eyes. "Dare I mention you've never felt *truly sorry* for me?" She threw back her head so she could look him full in the face. Her expression said it all without need for words. It was *true*. He had been very hard on her and they both had to contend with the fact that it was still eating away at her.

"I'm human." He shrugged a wide shoulder. Wide shoulders made a dinner jacket hang divinely. "Humans make mistakes. Besides, you don't feel sorry for runaway women," he gently mocked. "Did I tell you how beautiful you look tonight?"

She had him back. Was she going to drive him away again? "You did, a number of times," she relented, bestowing on him her sweetest smile. "But don't worry. I won't tire of hearing it."

"My first and my *only* great obsession," he murmured, his blue eyes aglitter. All around them, couples were dancing, slowly, sinuously to a familiar romantic ballad. There was no sign of Sally or her husband. Zara hoped fervently they would make up. Sally had embarked on marriage, from all accounts, to a fine young man. Surely she had to give it, at the very least, her best shot.

Eventually the music stopped and Garrick smiled into her face, noting her magnolia skin was showing the flush of intense sexual awareness. He imagined there was colour under his own skin. *Heat!* "Dancing is what tonight is all about, agreed?"

"Agreed." She laughed, a happy sound.

" So why don't we show 'em how to do it?" he suggested. "We were great in the old days."

"Weren't we ever!" She snapped to attention. "So what's it going to be?"

Garrick, his head slightly turned, was getting ready to signal the band. "A tango. Are you up for it?"

She grasped his arm, assuming a serious yet passionate expression. "Get real! We're talking about my favourite."

He laughed aloud. "Okay, let's show them how to do the dance of love!"

Across the Great Hall, half shielded by the luxuriant fronds of an enormous golden cane, Sally Draper watched the performance, a fevered shine to her hazel eyes. Longing she had thought buried deep inside her had broken free, gushing like a fountain for all to see. That public kiss had been a terrible mistake but her emotions had become too fierce to restrain. She loved Garrick Rylance. She had loved him for most of her life. Her parents had held high hopes for a union of the two great pastoral families. They had been thrilled out of their minds when the engagement was announced, although she knew in her heart that not only Garrick's parents had had some reservations. So had her own father.

"The cousin—the Rylance girl—what was that all about?" he had asked, his brow knotted in concern.

"It's over, Dad. Long over. Garrick has moved on. Be happy for me."

She shouldn't have come this weekend. Nick had been committed to play but she could have made some excuse. She had made a fool of herself and a fool of Nick, her husband. For once, he was very angry with her. He hadn't seen that kiss as a joke.

"Goddamn it, Sal; you're still in love with him?"

"Nonsense! The kiss was nothing!"

"Didn't look like that to me. Or anyone else. What you did was insane. I don't want to hurt you, Sal, but Rick isn't in love with you. He never was. He's crazy about that cousin of his. I thought you would have known that when you and your whole family went after him."

She *had* gone after him. No two ways about it. There was pressure on Garrick to get married and have children. Hopefully, a male heir first up. She had believed she could make him love her. How pathetic, how futile was that? No one could love to order any more than they could cease loving someone they couldn't have.

But that Zara was a callous, cold-hearted vixen who

liked to collect men's hearts. She was the quintessential siren. Just look at her now, showing her true colours. The tango wasn't a dance she approved of at all. Way too familiar and the movements—all that footwork—far too difficult. She disliked the flamboyant head snaps. She particularly disliked the overly close body contact. It was as good as a passionate embrace.

The guitarist was really going to town, his defining moment when the piano and the double bass joined in, their faces aglow with enjoyment. She knew Garrick was a skilled natural dancer. He had made several trips to Argentina over the years—polo matches, business combining pleasure. She knew he loved it there, the people, the country. Probably that was where he had learned those extravagant steps. He wasn't in the least inhibited as Nick was. Nick disliked showing off. Not that Garrick was showing off precisely. He was enjoying himself *hugely*.

Where had *she* learned her steps? Garrick leading, her following as though they had spent many hours practising. She could never have danced the tango herself. Its main characteristic appeared to be an overt invitation to sex. Everyone else had stopped dancing so they could watch this very provocative performance. Obviously they found it exciting. To her it was *hell!* She couldn't wait for the dance to finish.

And soon it was, ending in a very theatrical drop with Garrick holding that woman, her long legs outstretched, torso and head arched right back. Pity he didn't let her come a cropper, hit the ground. *Hard.* No such luck. Applause broke out. Wave upon wave of it.

In case some curious eyes were on her, to judge her reaction, Sally allowed herself to bring her hands together.

Briefly. She wanted to run out with a card bearing a great big zero.

Damn them both to hell!

At that moment Sally turned her head. And met her husband's eyes.

Sure enough, the party went on and on. Everyone was having a glorious time. And that tango! How about that? The highlight of the ball. Not long after Garrick and Zara had dazzled them, any number of couples began to have a go; admittedly not all that well but it was tons of fun. Especially the up close and personal. Sally watched on in disgust at the antics. No drinker, Sally got seriously stroppy after a glass of champagne. At this point she'd lost count. Who was counting anyway? Certainly not her.

Her husband was. Wearing an expression that was frankly pleading, he put a hand on his wife's slim, strong arm. "Don't you think you've had enough, Sal?" he questioned very gently.

"Enough?" She swung on him, showing yet another side of her personality. The determined to-hell-with-it side that won her big cross-country endurance races. "You're such a pain in the ass, Nick."

"Hey!" Nick, deeply offended, tried to remain calm. "I thought I was the guy you married? Why don't you come quietly, Sal? You have such a fine reputation. Don't want to spoil it. I saw Mrs Rylance eyeing you a bit anxiously."

"Uppity old cow!" Sally growled. "Guess what? She never did like me."

Nick was shocked. "She did too. Mrs Rylance is none of those things. She's a splendid woman and still a beauty. She's concerned for you, that's all."

"Go hang yourself, Nick," Sally said, further shocking her husband.

"Who'd want *you* then?" surprisingly he retaliated.

"I beg your pardon!" Sally made a swipe at him, hitting him hard in the chest. She was oblivious to the flurry of talk that burst out around them. Nick was a very popular young man. Far more popular than his wife.

"So you're going to make a show of us both, are you?" Nick asked, trying desperately to remain cool.

"No need." Sally reached out to pat him on his black jacketed shoulder. "Why don't you just clear off?"

He shook his head firmly. "You're my wife. Come quietly, Sally. There's a good girl."

"Yeah, yeah, that's all I've ever been!" Sally said in a sadly off-key voice. "A good girl. Men don't give a rats about good girls. They want the femme fatales of this world. They're the ones they're mad to bed. Like Zara Rylance."

Nick's expression changed to one of shame and anger. "Enough!" he said sharply. "Rick is coming this way. He says the word and you're out of here. We're *both* out of here. I've been friends with Rick all my life. We went to school and university together."

"Buddies, right!" Sally spluttered with rage. She had worked herself into a fine tantrum. "Is that his precious Zara coming with him?"

"For God's sake, control yourself, Sally," Nick said desperately. "You hear what I'm saying?"

"Give her a good wallop," an inebriated young man suggested helpfully from close by.

"Yeah, like he should try it!" Sally's expression spoke volumes. *Bring it on.*

That expression changed remarkably as Garrick reached

them, with Zara following a short distance behind. A very sensitive woman, Zara was suffering on Sally's behalf.

"Why don't we all go out and get a breath of fresh air?" Garrick suggested in a quiet but unmistakably authoritative voice. "It's getting a bit overheated in here."

Sally gave him a huge smile. She had beautiful white teeth. "Good idea. We don't need the other two."

"No. We'll all go out," Garrick said. "There are going to be a lot of sore heads by daylight," he observed.

"I don't want *her*," Sally muttered. "She can get the hell away."

Zara took a quick look at Garrick's face. He had already remarked that his friend Nick had better get control of his wife. Now his expression was set in granite. "You know, Sal, you used to be real big on manners. Seems you've lost them."

Sally flushed a violent red but she didn't answer. Instead, she twirled, picked up her unfinished glass of champagne, then hurled the contents over Zara and her exquisite dress. "Everything about you screams trouble!" she cried, stunning the onlookers.

"Oh, God!" said Nick.

"Get on the other side of her, Nick," Garrick told his friend forcibly. *"Now!"*

"I'm so sorry…so sorry!" The mortified Nick jumped to attention.

Helen, who had witnessed the incident, moved swiftly across the Hall to Zara's side. "Dear…oh, dear…oh, dear," she said, staring at Zara's beautiful evening dress, which was soaked in places. "What can we do?" she cried, clearly distressed. "Leave well alone? Have it dry-cleaned? Zara, my dear!"

Sally let out a laugh as if she was having fun. "She had it coming. Big time."

"You're a disgrace, Sally. No other word for it," Helen flashed back, brilliant blue eyes alight.

"Leave it, Ellie," Garrick said, catching Zara's shocked eyes. "I'll be back, Zara. Just give me a moment."

"What kind of a fool are you, Garrick?" Sally raged as she was being carried off like a wayward child. "Can't you see she's set to break your heart all over again?"

For a moment Garrick had no idea where this was going, he was so angry. "Shut it, Sal," he barked curtly, his whole demeanour radiating a possible instant reprisal.

Drunk or not, Sally was no fool. She did.

CHAPTER SEVEN

"LET me come up to your room with you," Helen said with a concerned look at Zara's pale face. She was quite composed, taking the distressing incident in her stride, but that magnolia skin was whiter than white. Mercifully, her irreplaceable evening dress was already drying out, with little damage apparent. Zara could be depended upon to act like the lady she was. There was now a big question mark hanging over Sally Draper.

Zara put out her hand, more upset for Helen, who was mistress of Coorango and hostess for this Gala weekend, than herself. "Don't let this get to you, Helen," she said, rubbing Helen's arm. "Sally was drunk. She probably won't remember anything about it in the morning."

"*She* mightn't. *I* will," Helen retorted, putting her own hand over Zara's. "How dare she? Like a bomb going off. Unforgivable. She's brought disgrace on her family. The Forbes are proud, very decent people."

"As Sally has been up to date," Zara pointed out.

Helen threw up her hands. "Considering how she behaved, you're very forgiving, Zara."

"Truth is, I *feel* for her." Zara was quite sincere. She understood Sally's big problem. "Sally loves Garrick. She married Nick. Just imagine what that's like, Helen! She really shouldn't have come this weekend, feeling the way she does."

"She won't come to another," said Helen, not nearly so forgiving. "I've never noticed before, but Sally has a manic side. If she's not careful, she's going to bring her marriage down on her head."

"I hope not. But it could happen. I suppose at the end of the day one can't waste one's life. Look, Helen, you were about to go off to bed. It's been a very long day but a marvellous success. We can't let one incident spoil it."

"Indeed no," Helen agreed, lost in admiration for Zara's forbearance. "I noticed a few of the guests were actually enjoying the action. Young Angus McKellar, for one. What was he hoping for, a fist fight? I thank God Daniel missed it. He would have given Sally a piece of his mind."

"I think she was too far gone to take anything in," Zara pointed out wryly. "Nick shouldn't have spent so much time away from her. He must be aware she's no drinker."

"I have to say, in all these long years I've never seen her like that," Helen conceded.

"Unhappiness can do it," said Zara, well acquainted with that state of mind. "Unhappiness is driving her a little crazy. Nick should take her on a long holiday. He has to be hurting too."

"Of course he is," Helen agreed vigorously, highly disgusted with Sally. "You're sure you're all right, Zara?"

"I'm fine, Helen. Truly. As they say, worse things happen at sea."

Helen gave her a beaming smile of approval. "Sally is lucky. She might have got pushed over the side. I don't like to leave Daniel for long stretches."

"I know that." Zara felt a flow of sympathy. Helen,

with all her worries, hardly needed Sally Draper to spoil Coorango's big weekend.

"Garrick will be back shortly," Helen said with relief. "Poor old Nick needs to get a whole lot tougher."

Zara's answer was very dry. "Garrick is tough enough for both of them."

And then some.

She heard the tap on her door. Didn't answer it. She knew Nick couldn't handle the situation without Garrick's assistance. Even so, it hit home that Garrick had taken over-long to check on *her*. She had come to believe *she* was the woman he loved. Maybe insult and upset had made her a little irrational, but looking after Sally appeared to have been his number one priority. One had to wonder about that.

What else could he have done? I mean, seriously, now?

Her inner voice struggled to make itself heard.

She had taken off her dress, hung it on a padded hanger in the en suite bathroom. Incredibly, it was unmarked and she had given it a very close inspection. She loved that dress.

Not getting a response, Garrick half opened the door, putting his handsome dark head around it. "Zara?"

"Oh, you're back!" she carolled, turning to face him. "Do come in and join me." She was fully aware that she was being propelled along by a free-ranging temper that was flaring inside her but unable to do much about it. Such was the female tendency towards perversity. "But please don't ask me how *I* am," she said sweetly. "Sally's needs are more pressing than mine."

Garrick closed the door. "You got that right!" he groaned. The light from the lovely Murano glass chandelier glanced off his clean, high chiselled cheekbones. His expression was taut with multiple upsets. "Like poor old Nick was going to save the situation?" he challenged, his eyes sweeping over her. She was wearing only a nightgown that, if possible, was more beautiful than the last one he had seen. Sexy nightgowns were a real turn-on, even if they didn't stay on for long. The light was shining through the silky ice-blue fabric, revealing the tantalising silhouette of her supple naked body beneath. Her wonderful mane of hair, dressed for the ball, now sprang wildly and in disarray all around her face and down her back. She didn't look *quite* like herself. Hostile was the wrong word, he thought. Aggressive, maybe? Zara, aggressive? His forever cool, calm Zara—aggressive?

Of course she was.

"But *you* did," she said to prove it, her great dark eyes pools of light. "I'm okay, as it happens. I won't put you through more trauma. Not for me to complain. My dress is fine."

He tried a conciliatory smile. "I'm glad to hear it. I loved it. The nightgown is terrific too. I can as good as see right through it. But be fair, Zara, my angel. What would you have had me do? Sally was like a hand grenade primed to go off. She had to be deactivated. And fast." He gave another groan, deeper this time. "I actually had to give her a shake to stop her ranting."

"Now that must have felt *awful*!" she cried with extravagant sympathy.

"On the contrary—it felt *good*. She was almost entirely off her head. The shake made her settle."

"Then I guess we can call it therapeutic?" she answered breezily.

"Zara!" he admonished. "Let's get to the most important thing of all. How badly did she upset *you*? I didn't hear all of it."

"You could hear what she called me, surely? Trouble with a capital T. And something about *I had it coming Big Time*. I hardly know the woman. Yet she appears to hate me. I'm only grateful she didn't resort to some choice four-letter words."

He gave her such an understanding smile that it turned her aching heart over. "Actually, she did too. I wouldn't have thought she knew half of them. I had to read her the riot act. My good pal Nick looked stunned so she's been keeping the bad language under wraps. You know, you'd never recognize Nick from the man he is on the polo field. All in all, it took much longer than we hoped before she was out for the count. Poor old Sal!'

She couldn't control her tongue. It was that sort of night. "Hell!" She, who rarely swore, decided to give way to a few swear words herself. "Poor old Sal be damned! It was okay to ignore *me*. Why am *I* never poor old Zara? It's getting to bug me. You'd think I'd spent my life having the greatest fun, adored by all. Well, I was a victim. You met my father." She pulled back, ashamed of herself. "Anyway, *poor old Sal* is just down the corridor. You can drop in in the morning to check on her. I'm sure she's expecting it."

He used his long-fingered tanned hands in a truly Gallic gesture of frustration. Let Nick worry about his wife. His hunger was for Zara, the rapturous pleasure and the enormous comfort her body offered. His driving need was increasing by the nanosecond. Couldn't she see that? "Look, Zara, I know what you've been through."

"No, you don't!" She was trying desperately to retain her cool. "You only think you know." No way could she throw a blue fit like Sally. She wasn't going to mention the letters either. She just had to live with it.

"Well, at least allow me to apologise for not getting back sooner when you obviously needed me," Garrick said. "But I assure you I'm in no hurry to see Sally again."

"What? You think they're going to start over in Zimbabwe?" she mocked. "I'd say you've had a lucky break."

His blue eyes had the flash of the finest sapphires. "So maybe I feel a bit guilty for dropping Nick in it," he said. "I must be stupid but I thought they would make a go of it. But forget that. They have to solve their own problems. Is it possible that *you*, of all people, are jealous?" He spoke softly, tauntingly, coming towards her with a natural male grace that could only be called sinuous, like a big purring cat.

There was no question he wanted her. He was powerfully aroused. "I don't think *jealous* is the word," she said, savouring her moment of female ascendancy. "I can't say exactly how I feel. Maybe piqued? Will that do?"

He reached her, pulling her into his arms in his wonderful unique way. "*Piqued?* Not a word you hear often," he observed, staring down into her face. "You were such a beautiful child, you would have dazzled Heaven," he murmured. "The sweetest little girl in the world. *My* girl. I want a daughter in your image. Two or three daughters, if you like. Our son and heir. I wouldn't ask any woman to run a vast cattle station. Why don't we go to bed? I adore the scent of you. It's like a lovely cloud around us."

"Go to bed. That's the answer, is it?" She tossed her head on its long graceful neck, determined to play out her moment. "You're very proud of your virility, aren't you, Garrick Rylance? It would reduce any woman to begging. You're really a paragon of masculinity. And a glorious lover. But *Sal* would know all about that. I have to step back from that one. What if she shows up?" She arched back against his encircling arm, feeling his strength, knowing he was only using minuscule effort. "She could well fall into a stupor for an hour or two, then get her second wind."

"You *are* jealous!" His eyes were glowing electric-blue flame.

There was such an element of satisfaction, even triumph in his voice that it only increased her desire to hold out. "I am *not*!" She couldn't completely claim that. She was more than aware of the fundamental insecurity in her. Maybe she was the one who needed the therapy?

He started to use the pads of his thumbs on her erect nipples.

"Oh...oh....oh...!"

She was totally exposed for the fraud she was. This was a man who could make her laugh, make her cry buckets, as she had done in the past. Now she was pierced by a Cupid's arrow of exquisite sensation. It was so ravishing it was hardly to be borne without giving way to involuntary moans.

"I think you *are* and I *love* it! My Zara is jealous!"

He was just too sure of himself. "Just you slow down, Garrick," she warned, truly flustered. Whether he did or he didn't, the fact remained, the core of her body had turned liquid. "I want to *talk*—" Truth was, talk was less on the agenda with every passing second. "If you think I'm going to—"

"Oh, you're going to all right!" he vowed, bending his dark head all the way over her, kissing her open mouth, his tongue moving into the moist clean interior.

His power was too terrible at times, she thought dazedly. She couldn't hope to win any sort of battle of the sexes.

No wonder she was worried about it. While she gasped with the rapture he seemed hell-bent on giving her, he began to rain kisses all over her face, moving down her throat to the cleft between her breasts. She was growing giddy with excitement, her legs and thighs trembling so much she needed his arms to support her.

"Oh, I want you," he muttered. He sounded for all the world like a man drunk on a woman's beauty. "I want you in every conceivable way. I want to mate with you, Zara. Just like the black swans on Coorango's lagoons. For *life*. I'll never let you go now you've given yourself back to me. You know it. I know it. That's *it* as far as I'm concerned. No about turns from you ever again. When I'm with you I'm a whole man. And you, my love, are a pearl beyond price."

What thinking woman would possibly argue with that?

By late afternoon of the following day guests and spectators had begun their trek home, with the exception of Sally and Nick Draper. Sally had woken up with a fearful headache and, doctored up with painkillers, returned to bed until well after lunch.

"Sally would like to have a word with you," Helen whispered after Garrick and Nick had gone out to the four-wheel drive for the short drive to the airstrip. "I expect she wants to apologise. She seems very contrite."

"I expect she doesn't remember much about it," Zara said, unable to find it in her heart to rehash Sally's offensive time out. "Where is she?"

"Still in her room. Poor girl needs privacy."

And a supply of major tranquillisers, Zara thought. "I'll go up."

"Don't worry, dear. It will be short and sweet. Nick

is terribly mortified. He wants to get away." Helen had a sardonic glint in her eye. "Get away *home*, I mean."

Sally was waiting inside the beautiful guest bedroom. She had her back to Zara, staring out over the extensive rear gardens with their magnificent date palms, bold architectural yuccas, the virtually indestructible New Zealand flax with their tall flower spikes and dozens of oleanders in fragrant drought-resistant bloom, white, pink apricot, yellow and all the crimsons. A dazzling show!

"Helen said you wanted to have a word," Zara called as pleasantly as she could. Last night wasn't the first disastrous encounter she had lived through and it wouldn't be her last. People were notorious for becoming irresponsible under the influence of alcohol.

Sally digested this without turning. "I—meant—every—word—I—said."

Sucked in, Zara thought with a rush of dismay and self-disgust. "I'd hoped you wouldn't remember anything, Sally, you'd had so much to drink."

"Ah, Princess Perfect!" Sally sneered. "The aristocrat! The Rylance heiress! You can never be sure who cares about *you* or your money." Abruptly she turned. She looked unwell, her expression bitter and, it had to be said, humiliated. Still, she was ready to carry on the fight. "I'm no good with the booze."

Understatement, Zara thought. "Listen, Sally. I don't want any more unpleasantness. You go on your way. I'll go mine."

"God, you must know you'll never go the distance?" Sally said, collapsing into an armchair. "This will *never* be your world."

Zara gave her a long focused look. "You don't know me, Sally, so I place no value on your opinion. In any case, it's none of your business. I know you're in torment but you can't blame me. I've made lots of mistakes and had to pay for it. That's the way of it!"

"Spare me the philosophising," Sally retorted with a great deal of feeling. "Has he asked you to marry him? *Tell* me," she burst out, rocking back and forth.

"Oh, Sally!" Zara was filled with pity. "Why are you doing this to yourself?"

"Tell me, goddamnit!"

A cool refreshing breeze wafted in from outside, perfumed by the oleanders. It gave Zara some much needed comfort. "Sally, I don't have to tell you anything. You really ought to talk to someone about your problem. You must know you have one."

A bitter spark fired Sally's hazel eyes. "The problem is and was *you*," she said with great conviction. "You destroyed my life's dream. And another thing—I hate the fact that you're a Rylance."

Zara looked away. There was no point whatever in staying. "Sally, I'm going downstairs," she said quietly. "I don't have to listen to this." Through long experience, she was able to retain her extraordinary calm.

She was at the door when Sally's voice stopped her in her tracks. "I mean you're none too stable, are you? Garrick told me all about your mother. Said you're the image of her. You know, super-sensitive, nerve-ridden! Committed suicide, didn't she, your mother? That's quite a dangerous genetic trait to have in the family. What might you do if your life crumbled?"

Grief she'd had to learn to live with stirred to full life. "I don't believe for one minute Garrick spoke to you about my mother. He wouldn't do that. So don't waste your time trying to come between us. Garrick and I will marry. It's what we both want. So let go, Sally. Get help if you can't do it on your own. Even if I weren't in the picture and Nick wasn't either, Garrick wouldn't return to you. There's only one conclusion regarding your short-lived engagement. You weren't really suited."

Sally, full of fury and a terrible ache, once more reacted violently. She shot out of the armchair, staggered once, made a grab for the nearest ornament to hand. "Ask Garrick if you're so sure of him," she shouted. "Go on, if you dare, you pathetic trusting bitch. *Ask him.*" The challenge rang out at the same moment that Sally pitched the objet d'art, a beautiful little white porcelain swan on its mirror-topped ormolu base.

Zara, trembling in reaction, threw herself sideways but the beautiful little missile did find a target.

Helen. She had heard Sally's explosive cry, prompting her to run the rest of the way down the corridor.

The porcelain swan hit her fair and square on the left temple. She gasped at the blow, the sheer shock of it, lurching sideways towards Zara, who caught her, putting protective arms around her.

"Get out of here, Sally." Zara drew herself up like an avenging angel. "Go now. You were in enough trouble without this."

Sally looked devastated. "It was meant for *you.* Never Mrs Rylance."

"You heard me. Go now. Your husband is waiting for you. Tell Garrick he's to come right away. Nick can take the jeep to the airstrip."

A short mad laugh broke from Sally's pale lips. "I can't take a trick, can I?"

"I said, *go!*"

"That's one screwed up young woman," Helen observed when she felt able. "That was eighteenth century Meissen, you know." She gazed down at the shattered swan. "I never figured Sally Draper for a dangerous woman."

"Unhappiness has unhinged her." Zara was staring in dismay at the still rising lump on Helen's forehead. It was a miracle she hadn't received the full impact right in the eye. As it was, she felt certain Helen would develop a black eye.

Helen started to say something when they heard fast-moving footsteps along the corridor before Garrick burst through the open doorway, his brilliant eyes sweeping over his mother, sitting pale but upright in an armchair with an obviously concerned Zara bending over her. "Good God!" His eyes settled on the lump on his mother's head. "What's happened here? Ellie, are you all right?" He went to her, going down on one knee. "Ellie?" He adored his mother. The best mother a man could ever have.

"I'm perfectly all right, darling," Helen said, summoning up a soothing smile.

"You need an ice pack and a couple of painkillers; I'll get them," Zara said.

"There should be some in the bathroom cabinet." Helen looked up.

Zara disappeared into the dressing room and, from there, into the en suite bathroom.

Garrick's angry eyes moved from his mother, who was looking in charge of herself, albeit a bit shaken, to the smashed swan. "Isn't that Meissen?"

"It is," Helen confirmed wryly. "A lovely thing. We've had it since forever. I never thought one day I'd get creamed with it."

"Oh, God!" Garrick groaned, thrusting a hand through his thick coal-black hair. "Sally ran out to the jeep like a bat out of hell. Said I was wanted here. No word of explanation. Yelled at Nick to take off. God!" he exclaimed. "Did *she* do this?"

"Silly question, darling. It certainly wasn't Zara."

Garrick's black brows drew together. "It was *meant* for Zara. You just happened to get in the way." No question—a statement.

"Ran into it," Helen said, accepting two painkillers and a glass of water from the returning Zara.

"Are you okay?" Garrick's blue eyes flashed up to her.

She nodded. In the bush she had learned that one accepted things heroically, or as near as one could get.

"Well, as okay as she *could* be under the circumstances." Helen frowned, then winced at the stab of pain. "I started to get anxious. Sally was supposed to be making her apologies. At least that's what she told me. I came up to hurry things along."

"Don't talk now, Ellie," Garrick told his mother. "That's going to turn black and blue. You won't be able to disguise it. What can we tell Dad?"

"I know—" Zara offered a possible explanation "—you were in the mud room putting something away. One of the upper doors sprang open and the knob—they're fairly big and heavy—hit you on the side of the head. The upper doors are about in line with your eyes."

Garrick considered. "Plausible enough, I suppose. Dad would never dream anyone would attack Ellie. He'll be upset, but he knows better than anyone that freak accidents happen."

"I'd say we'll have fewer with Sally Draper gone," said Zara with uncharacteristic astringency. "I think you should lie down, Helen. Give the tablets time to work. I'll get you an ice pack."

"Yes, do that." Garrick helped his mother out of the

armchair, keeping his arm around her. "Thanks, Zara. This is all my fault in a way." He gave a self-lacerating groan. "Sally was just a time bomb waiting to go off."

"Not your fault, darling!" Helen told her son firmly, using his tall strong body for support. "Sally is the one with the problem. I have to say, after this weekend I really don't care how she goes about solving it."

A full complement was out for the big pre-Christmas muster. The day had begun well before dawn but Zara was showered, dressed and breakfasted not that long after she heard the clatter of the choppers carrying in the pure desert air. Three helicopters would be in operation. The Bell belonging to the station and the two very experienced hired operators flying the relatively small two-seater Robinsons, cheaper to buy and maintain than the Bell. The big cattle stations like Coorango and others of the Channel Country with their million plus acres always used helicopters for mustering, such were the vast distances and areas of wild bush where the cleanskins liked to take cover. There would still be at least a half dozen stockmen on the ground to walk the mobs. Stockmen were essential to achieve a clean muster and control the herd. Garrick would be flying the Bell. A mustering pilot who also had extensive ground experience was by far the most efficient. These were the pilots who had a solid understanding of the way livestock behaved. No one knew Coorango's great herd better than Garrick.

Zara watched proceedings from her vantage point on the Udalla escarpment. The fronds of palm trees fell in long cooling shadows over her. The whole area was covered with small stones and some extraordinary burnt sienna boulders sitting one on top of the other with spent woody fibres lying on the sand around them and a thick ground cover of tiny yellow flowers that bore a strong citrusy scent in the shade. A couple of rock wallabies that favoured heights had come to join her, unafraid. It appeared she gave off no aura of menace.

The whole business of mustering had always fascinated her. Though not born to station life, it had struck a chord in her which would have confounded Sally. She had always loved Coorango. Loved the bush, the natural world, the wilderness, the extraordinary colourations in the vast landscape. Even the fiery red of the earth was incredible. She had thought it would be wonderful to be in a position to follow her lifelong desire to paint. People who knew good art had assured her she had a real gift. Her father had made endless fun of her artistic aspirations. Though it wasn't *fun*. More like a withering contempt. Her father had been such a strange man. She didn't think she would ever be able to talk about the crippling effect he'd had on her. Corin, her brother, knew. Garrick didn't know anywhere near enough.

Well, he didn't read the letters, did he?

Impossible to overstate the consequences of that. Her father had always maintained the public pretence that his daughter was his "princess". A fiction.

An undercurrent of friction was running between her and Garrick. They weren't talking in a way, but they were nevertheless able to act their roles as a couple deeply in love in front of Helen and Daniel. Both were absolutely delighted that their plan to get Zara back on Coorango had worked so wonderfully well. The fallout had started when Garrick had demanded to know what had accounted for Sally's fury. She had refused point-blank to discuss it. That hadn't sat well with him.

"Why are you always on your guard, Zara?"

She had glimpsed the frustration in his eyes. But how

could she bring up the enormously touchy subject of her mother's premature death, let alone Sally's claim that he had told her it had been suicide? Further, he had questioned her own mental and emotional stability.

With Sally of all people! She had never met a more aggressive woman in her life. Even Leila, her stepmother, would never have resorted to any kind of physical violence. She planned on replacing the Meissen swan. She knew she would never be able to acquire another one like it, but she did have in her possession a lovely late eighteenth century Meissen porcelain basket with pierced sides, stalk handles and applied enamelled flowers. She knew Helen would love it, even though the last thing Helen would have wanted was for her to replace the swan. Maybe Sally, when she came to her senses, would think about doing something.

Don't count on it. But Sally was his fiancée. They would have talked. Of course they would. Didn't the two of you talk for hours in those halcyon days together when mutual trust was implicit? Why not Sally? A lot of the talking would be done in bed. After sex, of course. No use denying that hurt. He told you himself he'd lost all faith in you. Sally would have made a very good listener. Why would a man keep secrets from the woman he was engaged to?

Despite the voice that ran constantly in her head, she couldn't allow that Garrick had spoken about her and her mother in that way. Visibly tormented, Sally had lashed out in malice.

So why not tell him what she claimed? Clear it all up. Once and for all.

She stayed for a couple of hours, transfixed by the exciting spectacle spread out beneath her. It was most apparent that helicopter mustering could be dangerous in certain

circumstances, swooping in low for one, but she knew
she had to overcome her nerves when she was watching
Garrick in action, either on horseback or in the air. This
was his life. Sooner than anyone wanted or had antici-
pated, Garrick would become master of Coorango. Daniel
was keeping up a good front but they were all extremely
worried about him. He had accepted Helen's story about
being struck on the temple by the heavy door knob. Only
a few months before, one of the house girls had broken a
bone in her foot when a porcelain door knob had come off
in her hand and landed with some force on her instep.

She had driven one of the station's jeeps as far into the
base of the escarpment as she could, then climbed on foot
the rest of the way. It was no great distance, but a bit of a
hike, especially in the heat. Going down was a lot easier.
The choppers had landed. She knew the men would be
taking a refreshing break—billy tea and the traditional
damper with lots of home-made jam. Garrick had told
her the night before that he would like her to join them.
She hadn't gone to his suite to spend the night. He hadn't
come down to hers.

So, stalemate!

Sally had done damage in more ways than one.

She drove into the holding yard, where she was greeted
by the loud lowing of the cattle already mustered and
hand salutes and courteous doffing of Akubras from the
stockmen enjoying the brief respite from back-breaking
work. They were used to seeing her either riding or driving
around the station although she never got anywhere near
the perimeter or the desert fringe. That would have been
more than a day's drive and Garrick had told her to keep
within easy striking distance of the home compound.

By the time she was out of the jeep, he had joined her. "Thanks for coming by." His Akubra was pushed down rakishly over his eyes.

"You asked me to, didn't you? Anyway, I wanted to come. I've always loved watching the muster. It's so exciting a spectacle. Any chance of a cup of tea?"

"Every chance," he said, turning to signal to Jacky Pierce, the camp cook.

A few minutes later and they were sitting in the shade of the wide spreading Red River Gums with their showy white summer flowering, sipping at mugs of billy tea with its distinctive flavour. "Oh, that tastes good!" Zara gave a sigh of pleasure. "Hot drink on a hot day, yet it cools you down!"

"It sure does." He had removed his pearl-grey Akubra, a very fine beading of sweat on his beautifully cut upper lip. She had an overwhelming desire to lick it off.

"Going to have a slice of damper?" he asked. "I think you'd better try a small piece. Jacky is watching you out of the corner of his eye."

"Yes, I am going to," she said. "I don't need any encouragement. I know Jacky's dampers."

"He's actually a very good cook. His scones, biscuits and dampers are a big hit with the men. He even makes the jam."

She broke off a small piece and put it to her mouth. "I wouldn't want to worry you, but I'm not much of a cook. In London, when we didn't go out, Miranda did most of the cooking. She's very good."

"An extremely efficient young woman. How are they?"

Several emails were coming in every week. "Having a marvellous time. Our Miranda was the perfect choice for Corin. They complement one another beautifully. And she's so clever!"

"And we're not?" He smiled. A pregnant pause. "I miss you."

She stared straight ahead to where a stockhorse was busy cropping over what little grass there was. "I miss you."

"We don't talk like we used to."

"Could we *ever* talk like we used to again?" she asked, a melancholy note in her voice. She decided to risk it. "Did you ever talk to Sally about me? When you were engaged, that is?"

His expression changed, hardened. "Ah, so now we're getting to it. What did she say?"

She expelled a quivery breath. "I don't want to make you angry. Flying the chopper is a dangerous job. I worry about you, you know."

"I know you do," he said. "But what will happen will happen, Zara," he said sombrely. "Look at what happened to Dad. He virtually gave himself a death sentence, saving a fool jackeroo—who emerged with a broken collarbone and a few cracked ribs."

"You would have done the same," she pointed out with a quiet shudder. "You look out for your people, just like your father. It's inbred. I'm right about that, aren't I?"

He didn't answer, but pinned her gaze. "So what *did* Sally say?"

His polished skin seemed to have gone a deeper shade of golden bronze. It glowed. The blue of his eyes was startling. He looked stunningly vibrant and alive.

"Come on, now. I'm not looking to upset you in any way. I'll tell you this evening, if you still want me to. When you've finished work."

"I'll hold you to that," he said firmly. "Sounds like you think it's going to put me in a really bad mood."

"Just so long as the bad mood isn't directed at me. Sally did quite a bit of damage, one way and another. She created this undercurrent that's running between us. Don't deny it."

"Who said I was going to?" He tossed back the last of his tea. Most of the men had finished their tea break and were already on their feet, ready to resume work.

Zara picked up her cream Akubra, adjusted it on her head. Her long hair was worn in a thick plait so the hat could sit more comfortably and more tightly. "I think I'll get my hair cut," she said. She had been thinking a side parted pageboy curving in under her chin. She had good thick hair to boost the style.

He lifted one strong tanned hand, laid it down on her cotton-clad shoulder. "You're joking!"

"No law against a girl having her hair cut shorter, is there?" she challenged, staring into his eyes.

"No law at all. But I don't *want* you to. I love your long hair. I love the way I can pull it all over my face like a scented silk veil. Very sexy. A woman's hair is her crowning glory."

"You mean you'd fall out of love with me if I cut it short?" She gave him a little mocking smile.

His answer had a faint rasp. "I'll never fall out of love with you, no matter what you do."

"No need to make it sound like a life sentence." She accepted his hand up.

"Life is a mighty long time." He gave her a twisted smile.

CHAPTER EIGHT

HELEN didn't linger after dinner. "I'll go and sit with Daniel," she said. "Rolf will be back on Monday. He doesn't want to stay on in Darwin any longer. He's devoted to Daniel."

"He's a seriously good bloke," Garrick said. "I'll look in on Dad to say goodnight."

"I won't disturb him," Zara said. "We finished our book. Both of us thoroughly enjoyed it. I think we'll start on the next tomorrow."

Helen patted Zara's shoulder as she passed. "Daniel loves your reading to him. You have a beautiful expressive speaking voice. So like Kathryn's."

"No wonder Dad didn't want to speak to me," Zara shot back from the depth of her wounded heart. She hadn't intended to say that. The words had released themselves as if they'd become unchained.

"He's no longer with us, Zara, dear," Helen, no admirer of Dalton Rylance, pointed out with compassion. "Your life is your own. I'll go up to my darling husband now. He never admits to it, but I know he's in a lot of pain. He took a couple of extra painkillers on the quiet." She tried to keep her tone level but the bleakness and intense worry seeped through.

Worry, in fact, was tearing at all of them. Daniel appeared to be fading away in front of their eyes.

They sat in the broad courtyard beneath a sky brilliantly encrusted with stars. The Southern Cross, with its four bright stars forming a distinctive Latin cross, was very easy to pick out. The Crux, revered in the Near East thousands of years before, had enormous significance in the cultures of the southern hemisphere. It appeared on any number of national flags—Australia, New Zealand, Papua New Guinea, Samoa, as well as provincial flags of South American Chile and Argentina. It was also on the logo of the Brazilian soccer team.

"Gauchos use it for night orientation in Patagonia and on the vast pampas," Garrick said as Zara commented on the glittering brilliance of the red giant Gacrux at the top of the cross. "Strange to think it was last seen in the Near East at the time of the Crucifixion. We see it as a Christian symbol but our Aborigines have their own myths and legends. In the Red Centre the tribes see it as the great wedge-tailed eagle's footprint."

"I like the one about Biami and Mirrabooka." Zara smiled. "Remember, in the old days when we camped out under the stars you told me scores of the Aboriginal legends. "Biami the Sky God and the wise man Mirrabooka who so looked after the welfare of his people that Biami granted him eternal life so he could watch over them from the sky. That's Mirrabooka up there in the sky, gazing down on us, Rick. The great Sky God Biami made it so. I think that's lovely." She lifted her long hair away from her neck, relishing the cool desert breeze on her nape. "All of us who live good lives will be taken into the Milky Way. Daniel has led an exemplary life. I don't think my dad made it up there," she said with a pang of sadness. As deeply as her father had hurt her, she couldn't hate him. Hate twisted the soul. She wanted no part of hate.

He studied her beautiful face, pearlescent in the soft exterior lights. "I think I've been patient enough. You might tell me now what drove Sally to pitching a beautiful and valuable ornament across the room. Childish is the word I'd have to use. Sounds like she'd better get help. I think Nick is having second thoughts about the woman he thought he loved."

"Who could blame him?" Zara sighed. "Would you want to be married to a woman who was in love with another man?"

"You think I haven't thought about it?" he rasped.

"I know." She nodded. "Sally is consumed with jealousy. How many crimes of passion can be put down to that? Doesn't bear thinking about. I made the mistake of telling her we've discussed marriage. I did so because I felt provoked. She totally lost it.'

"God, and what's the rest?" Garrick knew there had to be more.

"Isn't that enough?" She looked across at his handsome face, taut with pressure.

"Look, I can't solve Sally's problems, real or imaginary," he said. "She has to work it all out for herself. Hopefully, Nick will help her. He *knows* it was all over between Sally and me a long time ago. He *knows* I love you."

"You could look a little more joyful when you say that."

A brief smile touched his mouth. "I'll give you all the joy you could possibly want tonight."

She wasn't going to deny him. She feared she needed him to keep functioning properly. Yet she said, "Our sexual relationship, Garrick, is quite wonderful. It always was. But sex, even great sex, can't heal everything, can it?"

"I suppose not. And healing appears to be in order. We have to expose the dark places to the light."

"I think so too. But I don't want to bring up anything too problematic at the moment."

"There's never a right time, Zara. Let's hear it."

She experienced a sharp frisson of unease. "Did you tell Sally Draper my mother committed suicide?'

"What?" Garrick leapt up in a single panther like spring. "God Zara, what a question."

"You did ask for it," she pointed out very, very quietly. "Just a straight yes or no will do."

He stared down at her, a pulse beating away in his temple. "You talk about *me* having no faith in you. What sort of faith do you have in me?"

"You still haven't answered the question, Rick," she replied.

He sat down again, his tone firm and authoritative. "Zara, much as I love you, I refuse to be subjected to an interrogation. Can't you find something *good* in me, apart from being good in bed?"

"Words are such weapons!" She sighed. "I think the world of you, Rick. I've told myself over and over you would never do such a thing. But why would she say it?"

"I would think that was obvious," he said curtly. "To make you feel as much pain as possible. She's hurting. Why should you be allowed to go scot-free? Envy is the same the world over. A woman's beauty is greatly envied. Wealth is envied. You've got both. I'm very sorry about this, but it seems Sally is jealous to a truly sickening degree. As far as talking to her about your mother, the subject never arose. Nor would it. I hold your mother's

memory dear. You must know that. Even if it were true,
and none of us know for certain, I wouldn't dream of discussing it with anyone outside the people I love. I mean
the people closest to me."

"But surely Sally was close to you at that time?" She
sat very still, staring across at him. He had such a *glamour*
to him—no wonder Sally was having the greatest difficulty putting the past behind her and concentrating on her
future.

He grimaced; now he was put on the spot. "In retro-
spect, she *couldn't* have been," he said with an element
of self-disgust. "Even today, I don't quite know how we
got engaged."

"Mmm!" It wasn't rocket science to arrive at the conclusion that Sally, with the coast clear, had gone all out
to convince him she was the perfect choice for a wife.

"What does *mmm* mean?"

"It means, as a woman, I have my own view on how
it happened. Which brings me to a matter of the highest
magnitude. Your ex-fiancée told me you'd had serious
doubts about *my* ability to carry out my duties as your
wife. She said you feared I shared my mother's unstable
temperament. I was a *femme fatale*—her words—a *hothouse flower*—I was in no way suitable to share your way
of life."

"Oh, how I do love women!" Garrick cried, thumping
his dark head against the high-backed rattan chair as if it
were a brick wall.

"That's not hard to miss." Her tone was dry.

"I beg your pardon! I love *you*," he answered flatly.
"Believe Sally's mad ramblings and you'll believe anything. I don't know what dirt Sally thinks she's been able
to dig up. She always presented as very bright and breezy,
a thoroughly nice young woman—I've known her most of

my life—but Sally had a darker side that used to pop out at the odd time. Let Sally get hold of a piece of juicy gossip and she was like a dog with a bone. Not my scene. I hate gossip. As far as I'm concerned, it's a real sin to spread information that could very well be untrue. Anything else she had to say to hurt you?"

"Well, she thought she was right on the money with this one," Zara said crisply. "In time I'd realize I had made a bad mistake. And take off. Again. I'll never live that one down."

"We have to relearn trust, Zara," he said, his tone a little frayed.

"And how do we make that happen?" She gazed back at him, all flawless magnolia skin and heavily lashed huge dark eyes.

He thought those eyes held a world of sad accusation. "So we return to the whole terrible business of the letters?" he said soberly.

"I don't want to bring the subject up again, Rick."

"But it won't go away, will it? Those letters are an emotional barrier. But they're erected on *your* side."

That stung. "Why *wouldn't* they be?" she said heatedly. "I know the way I left caused you rage and grief and frustration but, had you read even *one*—a miserable *sentence*—you might have understood my fears and taken them on board. Sally is right about one thing—I *am* a vulnerable woman. No getting away from it. But there are legitimate reasons for that. I had a desolate relationship with my father. *Daddy issues*, in the modern jargon, but I continued to love him. My stepmother, Leila, only added to my problems. You never did see that. Very cunning was Leila. I let it all spill out in my letters. But you had to go and burn them, which just goes to show what a state *you* were in."

"Zara, I've never denied it," he exclaimed. "I *was* in a state. Heartbreak is a damned sight worse than breaking an arm or a leg. I admit it was really, really *bad*. I could only see your flight as betrayal. I've explained my side of it over and over. Maybe I carried my pride too far—"

"You certainly *did*!"

"Okay, okay!" He stopped her sharply, half turning his head, one hand raised.

"What is it?" The friction between them was instantly replaced by concern. Was something wrong with Daniel? Here they were, having an argument, when Daniel could have taken a bad turn.

Both of them were on their feet as Helen moved very fast across the colonnade. "Come quickly," she bade them. Her face, even in the half light, showed tremendous grief. Her voice was choked with emotion. "I fear my Daniel is close to the end."

Helen and Garrick stood beside Daniel's bed, Helen at the head. The lights were dimmed but Zara could see Daniel was in extremis. A once powerful man had simply faded away. She hesitated in the open doorway, not wishing to intrude on the family grief. But Helen turned to beckon her in. Once inside the sick room, Helen exuded a stoic calm. "Come in, Zara, dear," she invited. "You should be here. Daniel wants you. We all do. You're family."

Her heart lifting at the kindness and inclusion, Zara moved at once, going to the opposite side of Daniel's bed. Her throat was full of tears, but she refused to let them out. She had to be brave and calm herself, like Helen. She held Helen, her mother's friend, Garrick's mother, in the highest regard. Daniel's eyes were shut. His face was bloodless like an effigy. His body was not so much a shell as a wraith. He appeared to have passed into the merciful realm that lay between life and death.

"Dad?" Garrick put a gentle hand on his father's shoulder, speaking very lovingly. "Dad, can you hear me?"

None of them really expected a response, such was Daniel's condition, but Daniel must have heard his son and miraculously rallied. He opened his eyes, looking quite lucid—his suffering had not affected his cognitive skills, but he was struggling to find breath. "All present and accounted for?" All he could muster was a hoarse whisper. He looked first at his son and wife, then turned his head along the pillow to give Zara a smile that broke her heart. "What a blessing you've come back to us, Zara!" The burning light of zeal suddenly shone in his eyes. "You and Garrick must join hands across me. I know you share as deep a love as my Ellie and I do. It's our dearest wish you marry after I'm gone. No lengthy delays now. You have to make up for lost time. It's what we need and want as a family."

"It will be done, Dad." Without a second's hesitation, Garrick stretched out his hand to meet Zara's. She extended hers, realizing that neither she nor Garrick could ever break their vow. All things had become clear. This was their life.

There could be no doubt that Daniel was made happy. He somehow found the strength to place his frail hand atop theirs. Helen moved in closer so she could put her hand over her husband's.

A pyramid of love.

That was the way Zara ever after thought of it.

Daniel smiled again, gave a little shuddering cough.

Then he was gone.

Though his hand dropped away onto the coverlet, the

three of them continued to stand there, hands joined, as they bore witness to the passing of a very fine man.

There was great comfort in those joined hands.

Daniel Rylance's funeral drew one of the greatest gatherings in Outback history. Everyone saw such an attendance for what it was—a tremendous show of respect for a man universally liked and admired. They all knew the sad story that had brought about his premature end, just as they knew, given a similar set of circumstances, Daniel Rylance would have done the same thing again. Bravery was what he did, though he had always called it "doing what had to be done" even if it resulted in one's own death or certain injury.

Corin and Miranda came home, cutting short their long blissful honeymoon. It was no imposition. It was what they both wanted—Corin to offer support to his great friend and kinsman and, as an extension, to Garrick's grieving mother. Miranda had wanted to be there for Zara, who was the nearest she would get to a much loved sister.

There had been concerns about telling Julianne in Washington about the death of her father. Helen had rung Julianne's husband, Elliot Mastermann, to break the news to him first before asking his opinion on when to tell her daughter the sad news—before or after the birth of their child, their first. The baby—they already knew it was a boy—was due two weeks' hence.

It was something of a dilemma. They all knew Julianne would want to know immediately and would probably hold it against them all if they didn't tell her of her father's death. But she had not enjoyed the easiest of pregnancies. She had really suffered from morning—or all day— sickness, as she called it, for the first few months. Her health was being closely monitored. Her blood pressure was consistently higher than her doctor would have liked. She had been told she must rest. She and her baby were in excellent hands but even her obstetrician, when advised, thought it better to delay the tragic news.

So the decision was taken in the best interests of mother and child.

As Helen confided, "I had a strong sense that Elliot didn't want her to be told. He's actually more nervous than Jules about the birth. He wants me to fly over. So does Jules, of course. She loves her husband, but she does need her mother."

"You must go, Ellie," Garrick said. "There's nothing that can be done here. Dad would have expected you to keep to the arrangement. That was the plan all along."

"But for your father to die *now*!" Helen's beautiful blue eyes welled with tears. "This will be his first grandchild."

"I'm sure he *knows*, Helen," Zara said, though there was no proof of any such thing. Just faith. "I believe we keep on loving whether we're dead or alive. The birth of your grandchild will give you a sense of renewal."

"That's beautiful, Zara," Helen said, forever amazed at how like her mother Zara was. Kathryn had been such a compassionate, understanding person.

So it was arranged. Garrick flew his mother to Brisbane with Zara going along to offer the warmth of comfort and support.

"You don't have to walk me right up to the departure gates," Helen, flanked by son and soon-to-be daughter-in-law, teased.

"Not only that, we're going to stay there and watch you go through," Zara assured her. She knew Helen would never get over the death of her beloved husband but she was putting up a very brave front. "You've got to wave to us until you disappear."

"Will do!" Helen kissed and hugged both of them in turn.

"Love to Jules," Garrick said. "She's going to be fine, Ellie. She has Elliot, but she loves her mum."

"I'll let you know when I've arrived in LA," Helen promised. "Then again when I get to Jules's. Elliot is meeting me. Take care now, my dears!" For the first time Helen gave way to a few tears.

She kept up her waving until she disappeared from sight. This was the first leg of her journey to LA and, from there, to Washington DC. They waited until take-off, watching as the big Qantas jet roared down the runway, then lifted off into clear blue skies.

"I pray all goes well," Zara said, still clutching Garrick's hand.

Garrick looked down at her. She possessed such quiet grace, slender as a lily, yet she had proved a tower of strength for Ellie and him.

"She's her mother all over again," Ellie had told him with great affection.

He was coming to fully appreciate that the serene look Zara had developed to perfection was not only natural to her but also a way to hide her griefs. "All will go well," he answered. "It must. We'll catch a cab to the house." They were staying overnight at the Rylance mansion with Corin and Miranda before returning to Coorango. There was far too much for Garrick to attend to; he was unable to stay the extra few days that had been suggested. He told Zara she could stay on if she wished, but she had shaken her head.

Coorango is my home now, Zara thought. Her *real* home. She and Corin had never had a real home after their mother died. "I hope Corin and Miranda will always stay as much in love as they are now," she said, pressing her hands together as if in prayer.

"Count on it," Garrick said prophetically. "It's beautiful just to look at them together and see their happiness."

"And us?" She lifted her poignant gaze.

His expression was grave, bordering on severe since the death of his father—death did tend to bring one's own life into sharp review—but his brilliantly blue eyes exposed his heart. "Zara, if I know with certainty only one thing in the world, it's *I love you*."

For that exalted moment Zara soared.

Miranda was there to greet them as soon as the cab circled the broad driveway in front of the house, surrounded by magnificent rose gardens. "Hello. Hello there!" She ran towards them, all aglow, throwing her arms around Zara and kissing her on both cheeks. Suddenly shy—she didn't know Garrick all that well and he looked so imposing; his height, the way he carried himself so different from city men, an outdoors man, his handsomeness, his whole demeanour—she gave him her hand.

That amused him. Garrick dipped his head low to kiss her gently on the cheek. "Good to see you again, Miranda."

"And so lovely to have you both. Corin should be here any minute. I thought we'd stay in for dinner. You've had a long flight."

"What she means is, she's a very good cook," Zara explained with a teasing smile, hooking an arm around Miranda's waist.

The very real affection apparent between Zara and Miranda was another kind of pleasure, Garrick thought. Their ease with one another was such that they might have been sisters, yet they couldn't have presented a more striking picture in physical opposites. Miranda the platinum blonde, turquoise eyed and petite; Zara, much taller, long slender limbs, dark hair, dark-eyed. They could have posed for a caption: *Blonde or brunette?*

"I've put you in adjoining rooms," Miranda said, alight with excitement. "I expect you want to freshen up after the long trip. We're having seafood. Wonderful fresh seafood. I know you both love it. We hope it's the best possible news for Julianne and her baby. Which means for her husband and loving family." So happy and secure in her marriage, Miranda had all but forgotten she had been abandoned as an infant by her mother.

After that things went forward in peace and harmony with four young people who had a deep connection and liked one another enormously. Dinner, as Miranda had promised, was a delightful experience. It seemed to the greatly admiring Zara that, Miri had gone to a lot of trouble, although she assured them it was easy once she had settled on the right balance of dishes. No course was heavy. It was all light, delicious fresh food—stir-fried fresh crab with a mixture of sprouts and chives tucked into an omelette to start, followed by melt-in-the-mouth Tasmanian salmon served atop a beautifully dressed nicoise-style salad and, a little later on, a lime and ginger crème brulée just to top the meal off.

Afterwards they sat talking quietly on the terrace. There was so much to talk about. Later they decided to take a stroll around the garden before retiring for the night. Garrick wanted to get away immediately after breakfast the next morning.

"It's a pity *you* can't stay on for a few more days,

Zara," Miranda said, almost succeeding in hiding her disappointment.

"She can if she wants to," Garrick broke in smoothly. "I have some compelling reasons for heading back but Zara will benefit from a break. I've already suggested she stay on."

"That would be lovely," Miranda exclaimed, giving Garrick a warm smile. "We can easily arrange a charter flight for Zara, perhaps at the weekend? We can, can't we, darling?" She turned to her husband, reaching for his hand.

Corin took it, carried it to his lips. "Of course." It gave him a great sense of comfort to know his wife and sister got on so well. Both young women benefited from their close friendship.

"In which case, make it Longreach—" Garrick named a convenient Outback terminal "—and I'll pick Zara up there."

Zara lowered her eyes. On the one hand she would like to stay a few days more with Miranda, on the other she didn't want to leave Garrick; only she had the dismal feeling Garrick might have the need for *quiet*. He might welcome some time out. Could that be it? He was seizing his chance?

Her inner voice spoke with sharp impatience. *How many times does he have to tell you he loves you? So why then do you continue to be beset by anxieties that can only cripple your relationship?*

It was peculiar stuff in a way. Yet Sally Draper had seen her fatal flaw. Vulnerability. Once the painful subject had been raised, she found her mind had reverted to painful speculation on her mother's tragic death. She had always known in her heart that Garrick would never have spoken to Sally about it. But Sally had achieved her objective.

She had gone about the business of stirring things up, like a woman looking to wreck a relationship. That was the least Sally had hoped for—to cause distrust and dissent between Garrick and her.

Alas, as yet I haven't perfected supreme self-confidence, Zara thought. There had been too much havoc in her life up to date. Easy to talk, *move on*. No matter how hard one tried, havoc took its own time to go away. Sometimes people carried their own personal griefs and resentments for a lifetime. Madness, really, when life was so short.

They regarded one another across the expanse of Garrick's guest room, which imparted a sense of richness but with a masculine bent. Her room, adjoining, was of similar dimensions but decorated with a feminine woman in mind. "Do you want me to stay with you tonight?" she asked, aware that the question had come out the wrong way.

"What about you, Zara, my love?" he asked. Do you *want* to stay with me?" His blue eyes mocked. He was still wearing the clothes he had worn at dinner, but he had shed his beige linen jacket. Now he started unbuttoning his blue and white striped shirt, revealing a lean muscular torso with a cleanly defined ribcage. This was the body of a supremely fit man.

"I only meant I thought you might feel the need of a good night's sleep." Quickly, she tried to explain herself.

"Then you presupposed wrong. Plenty of time for a good night's sleep."

"I can easily come back with you," she offered. Though his tone was wry, it was showing an edge.

"And disappoint Miranda? No, seriously, I mean it, Zara, you deserve a break."

"What about you? You don't get any."

He shrugged his splendid shoulders. "That's my job. With Dad gone, I hold the reins."

She made a fluttery gesture with her hands. "Might you need a little break from me?" she asked with a little crush of the heart. "Things between us have been a bit strained of late."

"Well, one can easily see why. Taking the loss of Dad out of it, we had to deal with zonked-out Sally. I meant what I said, Zara. Having you with us gave Ellie and me enormous comfort. Now, come here to me." He held out his hand, waiting for her to close the distance between them. "I never cease to be amazed at how beautiful you are," he said. "Just possibly it's driving me crazy. You have one of those faces that could easily be identified, just from your eyes and arched brows alone."

"Genetically transferred," she said with a little sigh. "Beautiful as my mother was, inheriting her beauty, in essence, has caused me a lot of grief."

He considered that with a frown. "Your father once told me he thought you were *perfect*."

She felt an immediate surge of impotent anger. "The problem with my father was he used people," she said sharply. "He saw the danger from you. So he set to work. You were mad to believe him."

Garrick had to consider that neither his mother nor father had had any time for Dalton Rylance. "So using people was his great talent?" he asked. He had never trusted the man himself. Nor had he ever come remotely close to liking him, yet he had believed in Dalton's sincerity when he had said Zara, his only daughter, was *perfect*. After all, she *was*. He had thought the same thing. Beyond perfect. Everything in the world to him.

"He's dead now, Garrick." Zara's sober tones broke into his thoughts. "I have to get over all that."

"Time to make your peace?" he suggested.

Her lustrous gaze was intense. "I'm not that good. I'm not a *saint*!"

Garrick grimaced. "All right. Let's not discuss your father. I can see how much it pains you. But here's something I have to ask you. And then maybe I can settle."

She stared up into his face. The brightness of his blue eyes was such a contrast to his dark features "Rick, ask whatever you like. I knew something was worrying you, quite apart from your grief over your father and concern for Julianne."

"Zara, my love, this is about *you*," he said, taking her by her shoulders. "You and me. No one else."

What lay ahead now? "Go on," she urged, struck by the quality of his expression.

He was silent a moment. "I need you to tell me if you could possibly regard a commitment made over my father's deathbed as a form of emotional blackmail," he said eventually.

She could feel anger and frustration begin to encircle her. "Sweet Heaven, Rick! I can't believe you said that."

"It has to be said. That's why." He tightened his hands. "I need to be absolutely certain. It was pressure in its way. Pressure has been put on you right from the minute Ellie and Dad invited you to Coorango. They wanted you for their daughter-in-law all along. They conspired—it could be construed as that—to put you back into the frame.'

He was right in a way. But Ellie and Daniel had been quite open about it. Most importantly, they had given her her big chance to make things come right. She wrenched herself away from him, the hem of her silk robe swirling around her feet with the force of her action. "Certain? Absolutely certain!" she burst out. "Oh, I could weep for both of us. I really could. I *love* you, Garrick." Her eyes were smarting with hot tears.

"You love me better this time around?' he asked in a gentle but undeniably ironic voice.

"I love you. *Love you*." Her retort was uncharacteristically fierce. Her flawless white skin filled with colour. "You haven't forgotten, have you, we pledged ourselves to marriage before...before..." She couldn't go on. "I'm tired of this, Rick. Do you think without that promise I might let the whole thing go? Is that it? You'd think I was a serial bolter. The runaway bride!"

He let his gaze rest on her. "And what a beautiful and wonderful bride you'll make. It wouldn't be the end of the world if you went away, because I'd come after you. I'd bring you back. '

"Same old thing, isn't it? Same old thing!" she said in a driven voice. "Some things obviously get trapped in our brains."

"The answer to that, quite bluntly, is *yes*. It happens all the time. Most people hold on to issues from the past. It seems to be the way we're made. The human condition. I'm sorry if I've upset you."

"You have a gift for it!" The words leapt off her tongue.

He laughed without humour. "We can't wake the household, Zara."

"As if they could possibly hear us, even if we shouted. This is a *huge* house."

"Indeed it is. Very few people could afford such a house."

"You should talk!" she returned with sarcasm. "Cattle Baron. Master of Coorango and your million plus acres."

"Oh, come off it!" he groaned. "These things we were

born to, Zara. God, I never sit down and think, *look at me, I'm a cattle baron*, any more than you think, *I'm an heiress*. It's so much a part of us we discount it. Let's stop now. We've both had a long day."

She was standing beneath the big contemporary light-fitting that hung from the high ceiling and held her in its radiance. She was hugging herself tightly, as if cold, her slender arms wrapped protectively around her body "Forgive me," she said more quietly. "I have to admit to being a bit wound up." In fact, to her chagrin, she was on the brink of tears.

"Zara, please," he implored. "Don't cry." High emotion turned his voice unintentionally harsh.

She took it for male impatience, stopping her tears by swallowing them down. "No tears. No tears," she exclaimed, her lovely speaking voice off-key. "I know what a terrible thing it is to lose a parent. I know what you're going through, Rick. But you can't possibly believe I allowed myself to be manoeuvred like a pawn across the board."

His groan was deep and heartfelt. "You're a very compassionate woman, Zara. You and Dad grew very close in his final days. Difficult, not to say impossible, to refuse the request of a dying man."

She could see he had given a good deal of thought to this. "I gave you my hand," she told him in an impassioned voice. "My heart was in my hand. That *heart* is for you. Does that answer your question?" Having made her declaration, she spun on her high heeled slippers, moving swiftly towards the door. "Goodnight, Rick. I'll see you in the morning."

"That you will!" he agreed. There was such a decisive cutting quality to his voice that she turned to look back, her dark eyes like saucers in her pale face. "I'll be the *first* thing you see." A man of action, he went after her, this woman who filled his every need. His heart was pumping with the force of his powerful desire. He lifted her slender body high, walked a few feet, then lay her down on the bed. His bronze torso had tensed; his burning gaze pinned her to the double mattress.

Zara had to wait a breathless second before she found her voice. "I'll call for help!" Hard to say why exactly she said it! Female perversity, possibly.

"Call away. You said yourself no one can hear us."

"Oh, you're *clever*!' She threw her arms above her head, her dark hair fanning out on the crisp white pillow slip.

"No, I'm a man madly in love," he contradicted. "Cleverness has nothing to do with it." He stripped off his shirt, then sank down beside her, grasping a fistful of her silken hair and turning her face to him. "There's no other woman in the world for me, Zara. No one at all. Understood?"

"But you still think I might run away?" She whispered it, but there was challenge in her eyes and in her voice.

"I'll make you pregnant. I'll make you pregnant with our beautiful baby. I just might keep you pregnant." His blue eyes glittered.

"Boy first, right?" Her long fingernails were digging in a little to the firm flesh of his long strong back.

"What is this business of boy, girl?" he asked with extreme impatience. "I'll adore our baby as long as she looks like *you*!" His hand sought and found her naked breast. It only just filled his strong male hand, but her breasts were perfect to his eyes. To his touch. The nipples were already as erect as a tiny ripe fruit.

"I never defaulted the *first* time, Rick." She still carried the scars of his lack of belief.

That didn't console him. He was older, wiser. It had been perhaps, a young man thing—he had only turned twenty-five. Besides, he wanted no ghost of her father to come between them. Passionately, he set his mouth on hers, taking in her little moaning breaths.

One kiss was all it took to release the torrent of passion that drove every other issue from their minds.

It never failed.

CHAPTER NINE

MIRANDA was delighted to have Zara's company. There seemed nothing they couldn't say to each other. No words were needed for Miranda to declare her love for Corin, Zara's brother. It shone out of her eyes. It put the lilt in her voice. Happiness radiated from both of them like rays of bright sunshine. It was obvious that Corin's foremost thought was for his wife, Miranda's for her husband. "Sometimes I think we're one person, not two!" Miranda exclaimed, showing her inner elation.

"So you lay in wait for him, landed on his lap the minute he got into the limo and the rest, as they say, is history!" Zara smiled. She had heard in detail the whole story of that momentous meeting.

Miranda laughed, then momentarily sobered. Both of them had taken a refreshing dip in the pool. Now they had sought refuge from the hot sun in what had to be the ultimate in pool houses. Miranda went to the bar fridge, took out two small bottles of lemon-flavoured mineral water and passed one to Zara. "Garrick doesn't know as yet of my connection to Leila?"

"Not as yet," Zara, unscrewing the bottle, kept her eyes on her sister-in-law.

"He has to be told."

"When you think the time is right, Miri," Zara replied

diplomatically, pouring the cold drink into the tall glass on her side table.

"I'd say the time was right *now*, wouldn't you? Garrick means everything to you, I know. He worships you."

Zara wanted to cry, an uninhibited *yes, yes, yes,* but the words wouldn't come, such were the niggling anxieties skulking around in her. "I don't know that *worship* is the right word," she said, looking wry.

Miranda sat up straight on her recliner staring back intently. "Whatever do you mean? He *adores* you, really and truly."

Zara heaved a sigh. "I've never mentioned this before— some deep disappointment, I suppose, that I haven't been able to conquer—but I sent many letters to Garrick after I left Coorango, admittedly in unseemly haste. But the truth of it is, my father ordered me home. In those days I did exactly as my father said. He was a tyrannical man."

Miranda didn't look astonished. She nodded. "I've heard. Corin and I have long talks. Your father inflicted a lot of damage."

"That he did," Zara agreed quietly. "Corin was always brave. Standing up to him. I tried—I so wished for him to love me—but every time he laid eyes on me he turned away."

"Guilt," pronounced Miranda.

Zara lifted her dark eyes. "You mean over my mother?"

Miranda picked her words carefully. "Zara, no way am I saying what caused your mother's car crash was anything but a terrible accident. But there's no question your father accepted, even if he never acknowledged, some of the blame. Don't let's talk about Leila." She smiled thinly. "Only we *have* to talk about her, don't we? We're family.

Quite apart from the fact you're kin, you'll be marrying Garrick, the love of your life."

"The *only* love," Zara said.

"So, what about these letters—" Miranda followed the subject up "—obviously they have a huge bearing on your frame of mind?"

"He didn't read them," Zara said starkly, heartbreak in her voice. "He didn't read any of them." She stared away into the shimmering gardens with the magnificent turquoise pool set down like a jewel.

"He was too upset by your departure?" Miranda hazarded. "You only have to look at him to see Garrick is a man of strong passions."

"And a *proud* man," Zara said. "He could have read *one*. I poured out my heart and he never read a single word. For years he remained convinced I had betrayed him. I believe that thought still lingers. He loves me. But he's not sure of me. That hurts. Because Rick was so proud, we lost valuable years of our life. I want children. As you do. I want our child before I'm too much older."

"And you'll be the most wonderful mother," Miranda proclaimed stoutly. "Why are you letting this tear you apart, Zara? You're such a loving person. Can't you find it in your heart to forgive the man you love?"

"Maybe it's because I love him so much!" Zara agonized. "And the issue keeps popping up. He *burned* my letters, by the way—the sad outpourings of a traumatised woman. My father once told Rick I was the perfect daughter."

Miranda snorted in disgust. "He really was a total bastard. Corin could put Garrick straight."

"No, no!" Zara's protest was vehement. "I'm not going to draw Corin into this. If Garrick truly loves me he should trust me."

"Have you ever met anyone who hasn't made a mistake?" Miranda asked gently. "I haven't. We *all* make mistakes. Hopefully, we learn from them and move on."

"I know. That's the best way," Zara agreed. "Sometimes I think we spend more time looking back than looking forward."

"Then so many wonderful opportunities could be missed."

Zara smiled. "You have such an inner toughness, Miri."

"And I learned it the hard way. Can't you tell Garrick now?"

Zara gave a little wince. "Not good timing, I'm afraid. We had a visit from his ex-fiancée and her husband when you were away. The annual polo final and afterwards the celebration Ball."

"It wasn't a success?" Miranda's turquoise eyes opened wide.

Zara's smile was strained. "It was a great success in many ways, only Sally took the opportunity to vent her anger and jealousy on me. She still loves Garrick."

"Ooh!" Miranda pursed her lips. "How terribly unfortunate for her husband."

"And he's such a nice person too. But perhaps not tough enough for Sally. Under the bright, confident façade, Sally Draper is one tough cookie. Her outburst was so bad one might have thought she was on the verge of a nervous breakdown."

"Then obviously she must go after professional help. So she married on the rebound?"

"I almost feel sorry for her." Zara sighed. "I don't know how her husband missed it. If she'd given her marriage a proper go she might have gained a different perspective."

"I'm assuming she told you a pack of lies?" Miranda studied Zara over her tall frosted glass.

"I'm horribly afraid I took a few of the things she said on board."

Miranda understood instantly. "So you had it out with Garrick?"

"Garrick is the sort of man you don't *have it out* with," Zara confessed wryly. "If you start talking what, in his view, is nonsense, he hasn't the patience to hear you out. His verdict on Sally was—*zonked-out*!"

Miranda guffawed. "I can just hear him saying it! Garrick would have a short fuse with ravings. Some people have this dreadful destructive streak. You can't ruin your life over a sheaf of letters, Zara. I'm sure Garrick deeply regrets not reading them now. Going over and over this thing in your head accomplishes exactly *nothing*. What happened, happened. My mother deserted me as an infant, as you know. I grew up believing my grandparents to be my parents. Much as I loved her, I couldn't really *forgive* my grandmother for the lifelong deception. But I'm older and wiser now. I *accept* my grandparents did what they did because they believed it was in my best interests. *Your* best interests, Zara, are to move forward onto solid ground. Garrick is your love, your life. Coorango will be your home. Beyond doubt, Garrick adores you. What else is there to know?"

Zara turned her dark head, smiling with great affection at the younger and, in her view, wiser woman. "Are you my sister or my shrink?" she asked playfully.

"I'm both," said Miranda, reaching out to take Zara's hand.

Garrick sat behind the massive desk in his father's book-and trophy-lined study, looking with a sense of sadness and loss around him. This room was so much his father. His father hadn't wanted the big portrait of himself that hung behind him. His mother, so proud of her handsome, greatly admired husband had insisted. When his mother insisted on something she got it. It was a splendid like-ness but he couldn't swivel around in the plush leather chair and look at it now. Grief, of course. Nothing unusual about that.

He had been blessed with wonderful parents. Zara and Corin hadn't been nearly so fortunate. A stable child-hood, he had increasingly come to appreciate, was very important. Maybe critical. He had genuinely believed that, no matter his faults, Dalton Rylance had truly loved his daughter. The sick realisation that Dalton had played him for a gullible fool cut deeply. Of course Dalton had had his reasons. He was coming to a full understanding. When his beloved Zara had most needed his support, there he was, drowning in self-pity.

He sat there beneath the portrait of his father, clenching and unclenching his right hand. Zara's *betrayal*—that was the way he had seen it—had nearly broken him. He had believed with all his heart that they belonged together. Hence his bitter rejection of those follow-up letters that were still causing them problems. He had thought they would be the *Dear John* sort of thing, persisting in her attempts to get a response; the woman having the last word. His face set in a frown of self-disgust.

To distract himself, he began looking at the many silver-framed photographs that stood on the antique mahogany cabinets that supported the glass-fronted bookcases. There were many of him, mostly on horseback, playing polo and whatever. Almost as many of Julianne beaming at the camera. A lot of his mother and father taken with vari-ous VIPs and, in a place of honour with a widely smiling

Prince of Wales with his then wife, the beautiful Princess Diana, when they had visited Australia. Life could be a terrifying business, he thought, Diana's tragic death in mind. Without a word of warning, death could reach out of the darkness and take the people one loved. His once splendidly fit father had been left a shell because of a piece of random stupidity. No use to think of that now!

Lowering his head, he began to trawl through a pile of paperwork awaiting his attention. Once he'd had a good look at the contents, he would pass the pile back to Col Rourke, the station's office manager. Col was super-efficient but "the Boss" had to vet things first. Col couldn't make decisions, in any case, certainly not major decisions regarding the running of the station, but he kept the wheels well oiled and running. Col was an accountant. So was his wife, Felicity—everyone called her Flick—they worked together as a team. His father had employed them over ten years before. They were very loyal employees with their future carved out on the station. They had two children now, both boys, attending the station "one room" school. When the boys were old enough they would go to boarding school in Brisbane. He doubted if those boys would ever leave Coorango. They thrived on Outback life. Little bushmen almost from the time they could toddle. After a time, Garrick set aside the tall pile with penned instructions to be acted on, clipped it, put it into a folder.

Only a few days, yet he missed Zara so much she might have been gone for months on end.

You're lonely, man. Terribly, terribly lonely without her.

He had heard from his mother and Julianne several times. Both had sounded loving and upbeat. That had soothed his heart. All was going well with Jules.

We can't wait for Elliot Mastermann III to make his appearance. Hello, world!

Personally, he didn't go along with tacking numbers after a boy child's name, but whatever pleased Jules and Elliot; it was their decision. The Mastermanns were a distinguished family anyway. Garrick knew his mother had missed her only daughter. He missed Jules too. He wouldn't be in the least surprised if Ellie didn't spend a lot of time in the United States in future. He and Zara would certainly find the time to make their own trip over.

He had *plans!* Big plans—and they all revolved around Zara and their future.

The yards were so full of fat cattle on the cool calm nights he could hear the lowing and bellowing from the house. Even after long exhausting days of dragging, ear-marking and branding clean skins, he couldn't sleep. He was forever tossing and turning. When he did drift off, it was to wake abruptly, searching, arm outstretched, with the knowledge that Zara wasn't lying in the bed beside him. Difficult indeed for a man to settle without the woman he loved.

The night before Zara was due back—he was to fly to Longreach to pick her up—he decided to shift a few things out of his father's study and into his own. For a little while at least he had to reel back the grief. His study wasn't as spacious or anywhere near as grand as his father's but he planned on doing a few things to brighten it up. Zara had been talking about getting back to her painting. He knew she was a gifted artist who had turned her back on that gift for a career of rising brilliance. Her former career was over. She assured him she had no regrets. Time for her to take up her work again. He planned on hanging some of her paintings on his study walls. They could replace his collection of antique firearms, most of them untouched, from the eighteen-hundreds—totally legal—and his stock-pile of silver cups and trophies. So many, since his boy-hood, that his mother had put a lot of them into storage. As a family they were great collectors.

"Recycle them if you like!" his mother said. It was what she did.

He hadn't bothered.

Two magnificent gilded bronze sculptures of horses took up the centre shelves of matching bookcases on opposite sides of the cedar-panelled room. He'd had to have a shelf removed to accommodate their size. Another magnificent bronze of the station's famous prize-winning bull, Atlas, stood on a black onyx plinth. He might get the two big armchairs recovered. The fabric wasn't worn but it looked a bit tired. The room was spacious enough to place a big Asian chest between them as a coffee table, though he never had coffee there. Books on architecture and photography, a passing interest—he rarely had the time—sat atop it. Lord knew how long it was since he had opened the yellow rosewood chest. He pulled the sofa nearer it, threw off the rug that had been draped across it, then removed the books, placing them on the Persian rug.

A musky scent, far from unpleasant, mixed with moth-balls, assailed his nostrils the moment he opened back the lid. The first thing that caught his attention was a cricket bat inscribed by their great batsman, Don Bradman. He pulled it out, deciding on the spot to find a better place for it. He had been a very dashing cricketer at school and university. Fast bowler, but a handy, big hit batsman when needed. More books. Modern, ancient history, travel. A dozen or more photo albums. He would go through them with Zara when she came home. Another smallish antique rug he had folded away when he'd found the bigger, more stunning one that was here now. He opened the top one, ambushed by memories. This was his hideout for the countless photographs he had taken of Zara and she had taken of him. The old pain touched his heart.

Zara, oh, Zara!

Perhaps he hadn't opened the chest in so long because he saw it as some sort of mausoleum. Death of a dream. Well, in a large way he was responsible for it. Better close up. He had a mid-morning meeting with two of his fellow cattle men. Lots of issues within the industry to discuss; an overseas trade mission coming up. He wanted to check on the station's new mechanic before that.

Blind luck illuminated what looked like the edge of an envelope tucked into one of the books. A moment of premonition.

"What's this?" he muttered aloud into the silence, considering the protruding edge. An envelope, fine quality paper, palest grey. For another full minute he sat there like a man paralysed before he was finally able to pick up the book. It was very finely bound, burgundy leather, gold tooled. An anthology of the major British poets. Zara loved poetry. Keats was one of her great favourites, Shelley another. She had loved reading poetry to him while they lay in the cool shade at their favourite swimming spot, Blue Lady Lagoon.

Come on, man, what's wrong with you? jeered the voice in his head. *Don't have the guts to see what it is? Don't have the guts to actually open it?*

He felt his jaw tighten. Guts be damned! He postponed the moment no longer. He already knew with certainty what it was. One of Zara's letters. Somehow it had escaped the bonfire. But how had it? Whatever part of his brain that had forgotten or chosen to forget, his holding the grey envelope in his hand triggered a memory. Getting very drunk. A rare event. But he had taken a bottle of his father's very best single malt, sprawling back in his study brooding on his heartbreak long after his parents had gone to bed. No way was he going to allow them—indeed anyone—in on his heartache. Alcohol only numbed it. It didn't go away.

"I *nearly* opened it." Again, he said the words aloud.

He'd come close, so close…staring at the envelope with his name and the address of the station written on it in her elegant artistic hand. He hadn't destroyed it. He hadn't left it out on the chest so he could put it with all the rest. He had shoved it back between the pages of Shelley's *To Night* and *When the Lamp is Shattered*.

Kiss her until she be wearied out.

He had even bound her beautiful long sable hair with paper daises. He'd been a man "rocked by passion". Mocked and left. Then let it be so! He had slammed the anthology shut. Never opened it again. Alcohol had taken care of memory. Now he moved to one of the armchairs, paper opener in hand.

Oh, thank you, God, for giving me this break. Or is it you, Dad?

He didn't care that he was talking to himself. He was overwhelmed by gratitude. His thwarted passion for Zara had made his memories and emotions warp. A single saved letter could turn out to be his redemption.

CHAPTER TEN

THE dry heat of the Outback hit her the moment she put her head outside the open door of the charter plane. It had been a smooth flight. Corin had arranged it all. Garrick would be picking her up. She wondered if he had flown in yet. Knowing Garrick, he was probably waiting for her inside the terminal.

She had so much enjoyed her stay with Miri and Corin. It had revived her flagging spirits. Not only that, she had found real meaning in Miri's fluent comments and tolerant advice. So wise for someone so young! Qualities like that would make Miri a fine doctor. Miri had certainly helped her come to the full realization that it was a totally point-less exercise agonizing over the errors of the past. And that was what she had been doing. Repetitive patterns most people found hard to break. In her case, those patterns had been in play way too long. True love didn't reject. True love didn't threaten. She and Garrick had made their commitment. Garrick was her destiny. She wanted no one else.

All sorts of ideas about a June wedding had been filter-ing through her mind. June was a lovely month, the start of the crisp blue and gold period that passed for winter. She and Miri had actually sat by the swimming pool one day discussing the latest trends in wedding dress design.

Miri had told her with soft dreamy tears in her eyes that Corin had confided he would always carry the image of her on their wedding day in his mind. That was the way Zara wanted to be remembered as a bride.

"Don't let anyone tell *us* there's no such thing as perfect love," Miri declared. "Corin says he's a bigger, better, stronger man with me by his side. Isn't that lovely? I feel the same way."

She saw him before he saw her. He stood head and shoulders above the crowd that had arrived some ten minutes earlier on a domestic flight. His attention had been diverted by a stocky grey-haired man who came forward with a wide grin on his face, his hand extended for the usual handshake.

A moment more and Garrick turned back to look over the heads of the swirling crowd. Voices all around him were lifted in greeting—newly arrived family or friends. He knew a lot of these people. Most knew him. They exchanged friendly waves. He had long since accepted his pioneering family, and other families like his, were held to be something of Outback royalty. And, similar to the real thing, the position carried obligations that went along with the job. He was always stopped wherever he went in public as people—even those who didn't know him personally—took the opportunity to speak to him.

Zara stood exactly where she was, waving. To know he was there, waiting for her! Every last anxiety dissolved like shards of ice in the sun. She waited with an intoxicated heart. She knew she could travel the length and breadth of the world and never find anyone she could love more than Garrick. They belonged together. Drawn from the beginning like magnets. Her father had sought to control her life. Not a moment too soon, she had her life back.

Now isn't that amazing! applauded that voice in her head. *You finally realize just how lucky you are.*

He opened his arms wide. She ran to him on winged feet. Felt his arms close strongly around her, wrapping her in a powerful sense of comfort and security. Home to Garrick. No doubt was left in her mind. She would make him a wonderful wife; a wonderful loving mother for their children. Peace at last! And she had it. Mind, body and soul. One could only marvel at it.

In the cool of late afternoon they took the horses to their favourite haunt from their early days, Blue Lady Lagoon. With the horses tethered, Garrick took the lead as they plunged under the trees through a thick break of coolabahs then wave upon wave of feathery golden cassia—acacias with masses of tiny purple fringed lilies growing thickly at their feet. The whole area was suffused in a glow that one often saw when diving underwater—a cool misty green shot through with rays of honey-gold. Birds shrieked, whistled and called to one another, flashing their brilliant colours as they rose higher and higher into the branches of the trees. The reed-shadowed emerald waters of the lagoon shimmered before them, alight with a floating canopy of blue lotus, the exquisite waterlily found naturally all over Australia and North Africa and once the sacred flower of ancient Egypt. No wonder! It was fantastically beautiful in its smouldering blue-violet splendour.

In a euphoric state—this spot was sacred to her in many ways—Zara took off her cream Akubra and threw it unerringly to land on top of a flat-topped silvery-grey boulder. She lifted her arms, stretching them ecstatically to the blue chinks of sky that showed through the interlocking branches. "Oh, I love this place!" she cried with delight. "It's life itself! Isn't it, darling?" She turned her dark head and a low slanting sunbeam fell across her lovely face.

Garrick moved swiftly, stirred as ever by her beauty, both inside and out. He came behind her, locking his arms around her waist and drawing her against him, feeling absolutely complete. "It is!" He expelled a deep quiet breath. "But then anywhere would look infinitely beautiful with you by my side."

"Oh, how lovely!" She nestled her body back into his, still drunk on their passionate lovemaking of only a few hours before. Passion was magic, but a perfect understanding was the pinnacle of a binding relation between man and woman.

"Zara, I love you!" he muttered fervently, his mouth moving voluptuously against the smooth skin of her neck. "I should always have trusted you. I threw away your letters, God forgive me, and they meant so much to you. To *me*!'

There was real anguish in his tone. It made Zara spin in his arms so she could stare into his blue flame eyes. "Garrick, we have one another. That's the only thing that matters." She was struck by the depth of emotion he was making no effort to hide.

"You're so forgiving." He bent his head to kiss her. And then he began to speak in a deep, emotion charged voice, *"Alas! is even love too weak, To unlock the heart, and let it speak? Are even lovers powerless to reveal, To one another what indeed they feel?"*

"But, Rick, I wrote those exact lines to you in one of my letters. Yet another one of my appeals."

"If only I had opened it at the time," he lamented. He

held her one-armed as he reached into his breast pocket. "But the angels decided in their mercy to grant me a pardon. I found your letter tucked into an old anthology in my study. Long awaited deliverance, you could say, because in it you poured out the integrity of your soul. I must have left the letter there, tucked into a page of your favourite, Shelley. I confess I was in an almighty alcoholic haze at the time. Feeling sick and sorry for myself, of course. I took care never to have another session like that again, but sadly the memory of leaving your letter there vanished from my mind."

"But you've read it now?" she asked on a note of rising elation. Even *one* letter. Wasn't that what she'd always wanted?

"Over and over and over," he said with a profound gravity. "I can recite it for you word perfect. It's burned into my brain. I'm in a place now, my precious girl, where I *should* have been all those years ago. Forgive me."

"Oh, Garrick!" The glitter of tears was in her great dark eyes. "I do. I do."

"I have to confess to a tear or two of my own when I read it," he told her, giving her a beautiful half wry, half tender smile.

"How wise for a strong man to know *when* to cry," she said shakily. His words had touched a healing finger to her heart.

"And it does prove one thing." Garrick drew her body ever closer into his arms. "Miracles are to be taken seriously."

She offered up a face alight with love, with laughter and with tears. "I'll say amen to that," she murmured before his mouth came down to burnish hers.

Oh, the enormous lightness of being!

EPILOGUE

ELLIOT ARNOLD MASTERMANN III arrived safely, screaming lustily at the transition from the lovely peaceful cocoon of his mother's womb to a noisy, light-filled world. All went well for mother and child. Garrick and Zara were honoured to be asked to be godparents on the mother's side. The Mastermanns had candidates lined up for their side, including American friends.

Little over eighteen months later, Zara safely delivered her first child, a bouncing baby boy. Even as a newborn, Sean Daniel Rylance looked exactly like his father.

"We have to try again soon for a daughter who looks exactly like *you*!" exorted the doting father, cradling their precious child in his strong arms.

Two years later, Kathryn Helena Rylance made her entry into the world. Miranda and Corin already had their planned baby, their son Alexander, named after Corin's maternal grandfather. Miranda, a petite superwoman, was well on her way to achieving her life's ambition to become a doctor. Her babies had to fit into her tight schedule. Happily, they did.

Eventually five children—two boys and a girl for

Garrick and Zara; a boy and a girl for Corin and Miranda—
were to become the closely knit Rylance clan.

"What with all these children, we *need* a doctor in the
family," as Zara often remarked.

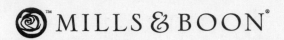

® ™ MILLS & BOON®

SEPTEMBER 2010 HARDBACK TITLES

ROMANCE

A Stormy Greek Marriage	Lynne Graham
Unworldly Secretary, Untamed Greek	Kim Lawrence
The Sabbides Secret Baby	Jacqueline Baird
The Undoing of de Luca	Kate Hewitt
Katrakis's Last Mistress	Caitlin Crews
Surrender to Her Spanish Husband	Maggie Cox
Passion, Purity and the Prince	Annie West
For Revenge or Redemption?	Elizabeth Power
Red Wine and Her Sexy Ex	Kate Hardy
Every Girl's Secret Fantasy	Robyn Grady
Cattle Baron Needs a Bride	Margaret Way
Passionate Chef, Ice Queen Boss	Jennie Adams
Sparks Fly with Mr Mayor	Teresa Carpenter
Rescued in a Wedding Dress	Cara Colter
Wedding Date with the Best Man	Melissa McClone
Maid for the Single Dad	Susan Meier
Alessandro and the Cheery Nanny	Amy Andrews
Valentino's Pregnancy Bombshell	Amy Andrews

HISTORICAL

Reawakening Miss Calverley	Sylvia Andrew
The Unmasking of a Lady	Emily May
Captured by the Warrior	Meriel Fuller

MEDICAL™

Dating the Millionaire Doctor	Marion Lennox
A Knight for Nurse Hart	Laura Iding
A Nurse to Tame the Playboy	Maggie Kingsley
Village Midwife, Blushing Bride	Gill Sanderson

0810 Gen Std LP

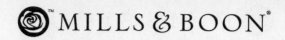

⌾™ MILLS & BOON®

SEPTEMBER 2010 LARGE PRINT TITLES

ROMANCE

Virgin on Her Wedding Night	Lynne Graham
Blackwolf's Redemption	Sandra Marton
The Shy Bride	Lucy Monroe
Penniless and Purchased	Julia James
Beauty and the Reclusive Prince	Raye Morgan
Executive: Expecting Tiny Twins	Barbara Hannay
A Wedding at Leopard Tree Lodge	Liz Fielding
Three Times A Bridesmaid...	Nicola Marsh

HISTORICAL

The Viscount's Unconventional Bride	Mary Nichols
Compromising Miss Milton	Michelle Styles
Forbidden Lady	Anne Herries

MEDICAL™

The Doctor's Lost-and-Found Bride	Kate Hardy
Miracle: Marriage Reunited	Anne Fraser
A Mother for Matilda	Amy Andrews
The Boss and Nurse Albright	Lynne Marshall
New Surgeon at Ashvale A&E	Joanna Neil
Desert King, Doctor Daddy	Meredith Webber

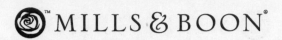

OCTOBER 2010 HARDBACK TITLES

ROMANCE

The Reluctant Surrender	Penny Jordan
Shameful Secret, Shotgun Wedding	Sharon Kendrick
The Virgin's Choice	Jennie Lucas
Scandal: Unclaimed Love-Child	Melanie Milburne
Powerful Greek, Housekeeper Wife	Robyn Donald
Hired by Her Husband	Anne McAllister
Snowbound Seduction	Helen Brooks
A Mistake, A Prince and A Pregnancy	Maisey Yates
Champagne with a Celebrity	Kate Hardy
When He was Bad...	Anne Oliver
Accidentally Pregnant!	Rebecca Winters
Star-Crossed Sweethearts	Jackie Braun
A Miracle for His Secret Son	Barbara Hannay
Proud Rancher, Precious Bundle	Donna Alward
Cowgirl Makes Three	Myrna Mackenzie
Secret Prince, Instant Daddy!	Raye Morgan
Officer, Surgeon...Gentleman!	Janice Lynn
Midwife in the Family Way	Fiona McArthur

HISTORICAL

Innocent Courtesan to Adventurer's Bride	Louise Allen
Disgrace and Desire	Sarah Mallory
The Viking's Captive Princess	Michelle Styles

MEDICAL™

Bachelor of the Baby Ward	Meredith Webber
Fairytale on the Children's Ward	Meredith Webber
Playboy Under the Mistletoe	Joanna Neil
Their Marriage Miracle	Sue MacKay

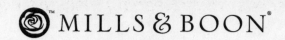

MILLS & BOON®

OCTOBER 2010 LARGE PRINT TITLES

ROMANCE

Marriage: To Claim His Twins	Penny Jordan
The Royal Baby Revelation	Sharon Kendrick
Under the Spaniard's Lock and Key	Kim Lawrence
Sweet Surrender with the Millionaire	Helen Brooks
Miracle for the Girl Next Door	Rebecca Winters
Mother of the Bride	Caroline Anderson
What's A Housekeeper To Do?	Jennie Adams
Tipping the Waitress with Diamonds	Nina Harrington

HISTORICAL

Practical Widow to Passionate Mistress	Louise Allen
Major Westhaven's Unwilling Ward	Emily Bascom
Her Banished Lord	Carol Townend

MEDICAL™

The Nurse's Brooding Boss	Laura Iding
Emergency Doctor and Cinderella	Melanie Milburne
City Surgeon, Small Town Miracle	Marion Lennox
Bachelor Dad, Girl Next Door	Sharon Archer
A Baby for the Flying Doctor	Lucy Clark
Nurse, Nanny...Bride!	Alison Roberts